THE WHITE SLIPPER

A CLEAN FAIRY TALE RETELLING OF THE WHITE SLIPPER

THE NEVERTOLD FAIRY TALES
BOOK ONE

BRITTANY FICHTER

TO SABRINA

I couldn't have inherited a better sister when I got married.
Thank you so much for your sweet smile, your joyful spirit,
and your faithfulness. You're one of my favorite people in
the whole world.

TO THE HONORABLE KING EVERARD AND QUEEN ISABELLE...

To the Honorable King Everard and Queen Isabelle,

Once again, Peter and I offer our sincerest thanks for allowing us to add our stories to the Fortress's library. I would be lying if I said I felt worthy of the honor, but since you have assured me that you wish to collect as many stories as possible, I am thrilled to add to your collection. The idea of having so many stories from all over the world in one place is astonishing, and the moment we're finally ready to travel again, we will readily accept your invitation to visit.

As for this first tale, though I've voiced my doubts, Peter assures me the story of the White Slipper is true. It was one of Tinker Bell's favorites, one of the few she was willing to tell the Lost Boys before they fell asleep. I hope you find it as amusing as she did.

Yours respectfully,
        Wendy Darling Pan

Once upon a time in a faraway land...

CHAPTER
ONE

River smiled smugly as she pulled the shawl off her head and shook out her curls. While her disguises didn't do her hair any great favors, they were a lot of fun. Almost as fun as the errand she was using this disguise to run.

Today's featured concealment was one of her simpler ones, just a borrowed dress, a shawl, and her boots. If someone had looked closely, they probably would have recognized that such fine shoes shouldn't belong to a peasant woman. But River was familiar enough with the ways of the court to know how to avoid scrutiny, something she could never do without a costume, of course.

But a simple working woman carrying a sack of linens was nothing out of the ordinary. And in the five times that River had used this particular disguise, she'd never once been questioned.

Sweat beaded on her forehead as she made her way

down the dusty road that led to the river for which she had been named. It had been one of her mother's favorite places.

The day was bright and cloudless and on its way to being extraordinarily hot. The dust she kicked up stuck to the bottom of her gown, and the wind that rustled the tall grasses on either side of her path mussed her hair. But in River's fifteen years, she'd never felt freer, and she wasn't about to complain about being a little dirty.

Ten more minutes of walking and a slight climb up the ridge later, the river came into view. The sun glittered blindingly on the water as it foamed and crashed merrily around the bend below. River made her way carefully down the side of the bank, slipping slightly in the sand until she reached the bottom. And there, beneath the large rock in the center of the bank, was her gift.

The leather pouch was nestled in the small hollow under the boulder. She'd brought it with her several years before, after realizing the rain could spoil the gift she was leaving in return that day. Since then, they'd placed their gifts in the pouch to protect them from the elements.

She smiled now as she lifted the flap. Today's gift was a round, sparkly river rock. River ran her fingers over its smooth white surface, marveling at how even the reddish-brown veins that ran through it were too smooth to feel.

River peered across the rushing water and shaded her eyes. Had he remained this time? In the three years she and Avery had been trading gifts, they'd never come to the river at the same time. This wasn't a surprise, though. Her visits to the rock weren't regular. She had to wait until she found a way to escape, which was generally once every two or three weeks. And though, as a second-born prince, Avery had a bit more freedom to go where he wished, presumably his father kept him just as busy.

But the challenge of the adventure was worth the effort escape required. Never once had she been disappointed. There was always some little token for her. Nothing fancy or expensive. A pretty stone, like today, or a seashell from where the river met the sea, or a few lines of poetry or a paragraph from a book scribbled on a scrap of paper.

But perhaps that was what she loved most about the gifts. Her life was one of opulence and luxury. With a father bent on spoiling her and adoring courtiers at her beck and call--and now that she was nearly the age to marry, hopeful royals with unattached sons--all she had to do was mention in passing that she would like this or that, and it was hers.

These gifts, though... They were personal, and they grounded her in the life she knew she was hedged off from.

"I'm sorry for taking so long," she said into the breeze. No one answered her, of course. No one ever did. But she liked to pretend Avery was there, hiding in the bushes to see what she thought of his latest gift. She'd never seen him do so, of course. But as his father's own palace lay just a few miles on the other side of the river, which served as a boundary between the two kingdoms, it wasn't unthinkable. "I've been taking lessons on how to properly set a table with courtiers who dislike one another." She laughed a little. "Be glad you're a boy. My tutor says only women get this kind of education because men don't care enough to try, and if they did, wars would break out like the plague."

The wind picked up, and River was suddenly aware that the shadows had lengthened noticeably. She quickly opened her reticule and pulled the parchment she had prepared. It was nothing impressive, just a few lines copied from a book she'd enjoyed, a story about a sailor who had spent twenty years making his fortune for the family he loved back home. But as Avery had often left her bits of his own stories, she liked to think he might delight in such from her as well.

Leaving the parchment in the leather pouch, tucked within the crevice to keep it from blowing away, she prayed he would come to fetch it before the rains returned. Then she picked up her skirts and hiked the sandy bank again until she reached the path that led home.

R iver breathed a sigh of relief as she slipped her dinner gown back over her head. Her return to the palace had nearly exposed her when one of the pages had looked a little too hard at her face as she made her way toward the kitchens. The weight of his gaze had caught her attention, and when she had turned to look at him, his eyes had widened. But before he could say anything, the cook had shouted for him to get back to where he belonged. By the time he might have looked for her again, River had slipped into the servant's passage and made her way up to her room.

"Beth," she called to her lady-in-waiting, who was fussing over her tea in the next room. "Tie these strings for me."

Beth appeared at the door and gasped. "Your Highness, why didn't you tell me you wished to change gowns? I would have helped you out of the other!"

"I'm perfectly capable of changing out of my gowns," River laughed. "I just can't cinch up the new ones in the back. Is my father back from his ride yet?"

"No," answered a smooth voice as a stately woman in a long, peach-colored gown entered the dressing chamber. "But he should be back in time for supper."

"Aunt Laura!" River hurried toward her aunt, forcing poor Beth to follow, dress ribbons still in her hands.

"I thought you were out in the town this morning," River said.

"Oh, I was. I was out with my husband, actually. Then I saw the most interesting servant leave the palace, and I just had to know what she was doing." Aunt Laura smiled a little, though her brown eyes narrowed slightly, and River felt her heart drop into her stomach. "She looked so much like the daughter of a woman I was once very close with."

"That's interesting," River said politely.

"Thank you for your help, Beth," Aunt Laura said, coming toward them. "I believe I can fix the princess's hair adequately. I would prefer you to pour the tea for us in the sitting room."

Beth, about River's age, bobbed a curtsy and went to do

as she was bid. River's neck grew hot as her aunt shut the door behind the servant and turned to fix her gaze on River.

"Just how long have you been going unattended to the river, my love?" Her words were kind, but her voice was sharp.

River sighed and turned toward her vanity. "How did you know it was me?"

Aunt Laura snorted delicately. "I hope I would know my sister's child, no matter what she was wearing." She began to brush River's hair. "So," she continued more gently, "are you going to tell me what you were doing?"

River sighed. "Three years ago, after my mother died, I would go down to the river and imagine she was still there."

Aunt Laura smiled as she began to braid River's hair. "She loved that river long before she became queen. Your grandfather finally gave up trying to keep her away from it and sent a footman with her instead."

River nodded. "I went to visit it every week. But I knew my father wouldn't let me go alone...like I needed to be. So I started sneaking out."

"And your father would have been right to worry. Can you imagine how easy it would have been for an enemy to kidnap a twelve-year-old girl?" Her aunt pressed her lips together, then sighed. "But I do understand."

"I ran into Avery there a few weeks after I started going," River continued. "We talked for a little. And after that, he started leaving me presents." She smiled in spite of herself. "And I would leave presents for him, too. Nothing big. Pretty rocks or little sweets. Once, he left me a whistle carved out of wood."

"Well, I'm glad to hear it's the son of your father's closest friend and not some vagabond set on kidnapping you," her aunt said as she began pinning gems into River's hair. "Nevertheless, I'd feel better if you–don't look at me like that. I was going to say I'd feel better if you would at least tell me when you're about to set out on these little treks." She gave River a knowing smile in the mirror and put her hands on her hips. "I may only have married a duke, and I'm certainly not your mother, but I would feel better if I knew where you were if I arrived here one day and no one could find you."

River grinned back sheepishly. "I never know for sure when I'll get to slip away." She looked around her desk. "What if I leave a signal for you when I go? Maybe..." She paused and picked up a quill. "I'll leave this on my pillow. Then you'll at least know where I've gone."

A loud banging on the door in the adjoining room made them both jump. Beth scurried in to open it.

"What do you mean making such a racket on the princess's–" she began, but she was cut off.

"There's been an accident!" River recognized the voice of her personal guard, Stephan. "The king's been gravely injured!"

CHAPTER
TWO

River didn't remember jumping up or outstripping the guards as she ran to her father's room. All she remembered after that day was waiting for an eternity outside his bedchamber, her aunt holding her hand and praying quietly with her while the sound of many physicians' voices came through the door in a confused muddle.

"What happened?" Aunt Laura asked Stephan in a low voice.

"He hadn't planned to go hunting," Stephan answered in a low voice, "but he was out with a few of his dukes, and one of them suggested that it was a lovely day for a hunt. He agreed and had his hunting gear sent for. Unfortunately, they forgot to bring hunting boots, and he thought it inconsequential." Stephan paused and lowered his voice. "He was walking beside the horse when he accidentally stepped on a trap. It went through his shoe and into his foot."

"Do they expect him to live?" River asked.

Aunt Laura and Stephan looked down at River, their faces taut. River squared her shoulders. "Do they expect him to live?" she asked again, louder this time, willing her voice not to tremble as it was.

"They're...not sure, Your Highness." Stephan bowed his head. "That's what they're deliberating on now."

River took a long, slow breath. She had lost her mother when she was twelve, and the following year had felt like a nightmare. She'd walked around as though in a fog, never able to escape the horror she awakened to daily.

At first, she'd thought the pain could never lessen. She would never be able to go on. But her father's careful attention, her aunt's constant vigilance, and her then-weekly trips to the river had slowly, painfully pulled her from the pit of despondence she'd been trapped in. But healing had been a struggle, and a great many days had passed before she'd begun to feel as though life might go on.

And now, three years later, to lose her father...

"River?" Aunt Laura squeezed her hand. River looked up to see her aunt's carefully arranged expression. "The physicians say your father will see you now."

River walked to her father's door in a daze. She'd wanted nothing more than to join him since hearing of his accident, to see and touch him and assure herself that he was still alive. But even as she walked, a cold fear slithered in, whispering that any minute, he could be stolen from her as well.

She stopped on the threshold.

He was laid out on the bed, his large frame taking up a good deal of it. Blankets had been piled on every part of him except his leg, which was held up in some sort of contraption that kept it raised above the rest of his body. His face was pallid, and the whites of his eyes bright red. And though he was the tallest man in the court and one of the strongest, he suddenly seemed fragile and sickly.

"Well," he said breathlessly before swallowing. "If you've come for a grand scene, I'm not sure I can provide you one." He trembled slightly, but there was a twinkle in his eye.

With a cry, River threw herself at her father's bedside. She clutched at his shirt as she began to sob through no accord of her own.

"Now come, River," he said gently, wiping her tears away with shaking hands. "No need to weep as though I'm dead. You're not free of me that easily."

His attempt at humor only made River cry harder, to which he responded by rubbing her back and continuing to whisper gentle words, as though she were a spooked horse. Finally, when there were no more tears to cry, he smiled and touched her cheek.

"This isn't like it was with your mother. She was sick for a long time. I'm as healthy as a team of oxen."

"What are they going to do about it?" River gave a sniffle, which turned into a hiccup.

The king flinched as he reached over to his bedside table and lifted a chalice of water which he then gave to her. She drank greedily, realizing that she was parched. Was it because of her walk out to the river that afternoon? Or because she'd cried nearly every drop of water in the world?

"This is beyond our physicians' scope of knowledge, I'm afraid," he said slowly. "But I don't want you to fret. They're summoning every physician in our land and inviting those in our neighboring kingdoms." He tapped her nose. "Promise me you won't fret?"

She glared at him through wet lashes. "Only if you promise to get better."

The king smiled, and River was relieved to see that even in his pain, his smile lit up his bearded face just as it always had. "I thought you were going to exact some impossible promise, seeing as you seem to think this is my deathbed."

She quirked one brow. "Let me plan your birthday party this year."

At this, he fell back into the pillow and roared with laughter before wincing in pain. After a moment of grinding his teeth and breathing heavily, he finally opened his eyes again, panting.

"I'm sorry," River said, but he just ran his hand over her golden curls and gave her a tired smile.

"My pain is not your fault, my love. And no, you can't plan my birthday. You'd plan some sort of ridiculous frippery as though I were some dandy."

"I would make it fitting for a king."

He chuckled again at her scowl, then took another shaky breath. "No, my love. Not this year. But I will promise to get better. How's that?" He took her face into his hand, and she leaned into his palm.

"Then that is enough for me."

THREE

Unfortunately, River's peace about the situation was not as sure as she had hoped. The king's recovery, which the doctors had hoped would be quick, stretched from days to weeks to months. The infection festered, and he was unable to leave his bed unless carried on a stretcher. And even that was painful.

River watched as physicians—not only from their kingdoms but from the kingdoms around them—streamed in. The king had promised a great reward for the man who could heal him. Unfortunately, the physicians seemed to stream out as fast as they came, and the king was not healed.

River was at her father's side for most of the physicians' visits. Ointments, elixirs, salves, teas, and exotic foods were prescribed. But none brought even the smallest amount of relief. And the king's bright, cheery face lost its shine, instead looking haggard and pale.

Sleep was difficult for both of them. For River had insisted on having a cot moved in to be kept at the foot of his bed, and though her servants and even her aunt deplored it, she refused to sleep in her own chambers.

"I would never forgive myself if something happened to him while someone else fell asleep," she told her aunt, two months after the incident.

"But you need sleep as well," her aunt had argued. "If something happens to the kingdom, you're all the kingdom will have left."

"I'll not even think of that now," River retorted. "I am his daughter, and this is my duty."

The only times in which River could be persuaded to leave her father's chamber were to change and to have her walks to the river, which she had begun to make weekly once again. And these she only made because her father, in one of his moments of greater lucidity, ordered her outside.

"You look as though you haven't seen the sun," he'd gasped out in pain one day. "Flowers can't thrive without the sun."

"I don't need the sun," she'd assured him, holding his teacup to his lips. "I need you."

"Well, you won't serve me well if you're withered away." Her father had pushed the tea away. "You're to go outside right now. And that's an order."

To his credit, her father had been right. Once River had renewed her walks, she began to feel somewhat like herself again. And finding her little gifts weekly, rather than intermittently, bolstered her courage. Avery, it seemed, was aware of her pain, for she never went to the river without finding something new to make her smile. And as the gifts were never water-stained or ruined, she could only surmise that he must come often to ensure they were delivered without ruin.

But as time passed, even with her gifts and her walks, her growing anxiety began to make River despair of her father ever finding healing again.

Even worse than her own anxieties, however, were those of her father's servants. And their fear did nothing to comfort her. Once, when she was trying to nap on her cot, she overheard her father's steward talking to her personal guard.

"I'm afraid the matters of state cannot continue like this forever," the steward was whispering.

"What do you mean?" Stephan asked. By the sound of his armor clinking, she knew he was turning to look at her.

"I mean that if the king can't resume his duties soon, River will need to assume more than we had anticipated."

They were both quiet for a moment, and River did her best to breathe as though she were really asleep. Her mind, however, was anything but quiet. Fear threatened to choke her.

"She won't be sixteen for another eight months," Stephan finally said. "Putting that kind of weight on a girl of that age—"

"Other monarchs have been crowned younger," the steward said with a sigh. "Not that I wish it, of course. But we don't have much time."

River didn't nap that afternoon. She tried, to be sure, as a brief escape from the world was suddenly her greatest desire. But try as she might, she couldn't get the steward's words out of her head.

Acting queen? At age fifteen?

Of course she'd been trained in the arts of economy and diplomacy. And she had a fair hand at speaking with her people, for her father had ensured that she was as familiar with them as a royal could be. But to be taking on the duties of a queen, even without the official title...

She wasn't ready.

"River?"

River gave a start. She was sitting at the edge of her father's bed, holding his hand as yet another physician examined his foot.

"What were you daydreaming of?" the king asked with a strained smile. A drop of sweat ran down his temple.

River reached over with a handkerchief to wipe it away. "I was thinking about the future," she said, forcing a smile.

"No man will ever be good enough for you." Her father tightened his grip on her hand. "I was telling your aunt that yesterday while you were out on your walk." He cringed as the physician gave him a prod.

"Tell me what you were talking about," River said quickly. "I'm sorry I wasn't attending." Not that she was greatly interested in her father's conversation with her aunt about her future husband. Marriage was the last subject on her mind now. But talking, she had found, was a good way to distract her father when he was in pain. He loved to talk.

He took a deep breath. "I was telling her how you will only marry the best of men."

"Someone I love, I hope." She gave him what she hoped was a teasing smile.

"Only to someone you love. And he shall have to adore you."

"Your Majesty?"

River and her father looked down at the physician standing at the foot of his bed.

The man was not a local physician. He spoke with an accent like those of their neighbors to the east. River had heard whispers that he was said to be one of the greatest physicians in the world, but she had refused to let herself hope before he arrived.

"I cannot heal you," the physician said gently, wiping his hands on a rag as he stood. "And I'm sorry for that."

River let out a deep sigh, but to her surprise, the physician smiled kindly at her.

"But I can make the pain bearable. Well enough, I'll wager, that you'll be able to walk again without difficulty."

The king pushed himself into a higher sitting position, but River sat frozen in silence.

"How so?" the king asked. "If you could do even this, I would gift you half my kingdom."

"I have no need for such hefty promises, I assure you," the physician said. "This is not a new remedy. It's not even a remedy at all, but an ancient treatment passed down in my family from one generation to the next."

"What is it?" River asked, leaning forward. Her heart raced, and her tired, muddled mind was suddenly clear.

The physician chuckled. "I'm afraid I'm sworn to secrecy. That we're aware of, no one in our family has shared it in four hundred years. But I shall make it for your father, nevertheless, Princess, and you shall see its fruit as well."

T hen and there, the physician pulled out a block of wood and a knife. The wood, which he let River touch, was soft and smooth, and nearly as white as an egg.

"It's a particular kind of balsam," the physician said. "No other balsam will do what this one can."

"It's so lightweight!" she cried in delight. "I'd say a reed basket weighs more!"

The physician chuckled and took the block of wood back, then he began to cut. In less than an hour, River could see the outline of a shoe taking shape. She didn't say anything, however, for fear of getting her father's hopes up, until the physician put his knife away and announced that he was done.

"Wear this, Your Majesty," he said, placing the shoe on the king's mangled foot, "and you should be able to walk immediately."

The king stared at the shoe for a long moment, seeming unsure whether to believe the physician or have him thrown out for playing tricks. But when the physician finally convinced the king to stand, he let out a shout.

"It's true!" Her father walked to the door and back, cautiously at first, then quickly, then confidently. The steward and the attending servants gaped. River felt tears running down her face as she laughed.

"Please, sir," the king said, turning to the physician, who was packing his things. "Stay for supper. Let me thank you properly. My entire kingdom will wish to see you and pay their respects as well. You've saved not only my life and my family, but my entire people." He held his hands up then dropped them helplessly. "I owe you everything."

"I will certainly stay for supper," the physician said with a smile. "But I'm afraid I have no need of riches or grandeur. My usual sum will do. And then I will be off in the morning."

That night, as River went to sleep in her own bed in her own chambers for the first time in months, she felt as though the weight of the world had fallen from her shoulders when she'd changed out of her evening gown and into her nightdress. Her father was better. The kingdom could flourish again.

And queenship would have to wait.

TWO YEARS LATER...

FOUR

River smiled down at the dried rosebud in her hand. The flower was tiny, just about the size of her thumb. But whoever had dried it had prevented the purple from dulling the way dried flowers usually did. And of its beauty, River had never seen the like.

"You're getting to know me a little too well, I think," she said aloud. No one answered, of course. No one but the babbling water and the twittering birds and the cicadas, which seemed desirous of driving everyone in the valley deaf. "I never told you my favorite color." Not that she really needed to. She wore purple every chance she got. Avery would have figured that out by now.

"I don't think I ever told you the story...No. We couldn't have. We didn't even tell the court. Unless the dressmaker told them." She paused and shook her head. "When I was eight, my mother told our dressmaker to make my new gowns any color *except* purple because she knew I'd find a way to wear it anyhow." River chuckled. "She was right. Per my pleading, my grandparents showed up at my next birthday party with not one but three dresses in varying shades of violet."

Then River sighed and rearranged herself on the rock. The day was pleasantly warm without being hot. A sign of the winter to come, her father's advisers had warned. Early autumn or not, River's aunt might die of scandal if she were to see River's uncovered face basking in the bright morning sun.

River could imagine the lecture now. *For all that's good and orderly, you're nearly eighteen! You'll be a wife soon enough with children of your own to cover! And yet, you're still leaving your nose to freckle!*

"I rather like my freckles," River sniffed to herself. Then she paused. "Did I tell you I've been granted the privilege to throw my father's birthday celebration?"

Again, no one answered. Avery was never there this time of day. In fact, River had never once seen him when she'd gone to exchange their gifts. That was part of the fun, though. Hiding the gift and knowing he'd find it later, leaving one for her in return.

"Aunt was skeptical, but in the end, she decided that I'm ready, and Father knew better than to argue. But if I'm honest..." She paused. If she was honest...what did she mean to say? She spoke more slowly this time. "I mean, I asked for the privilege. But I think it was to prove to myself that I can do this. Not even so much to them. Because I really don't know..." She let the words trail off again, suddenly grateful that her friend wasn't there to hear her. What a lot of nonsense she was jabbering on about.

"I'm glad to hear that you'll be there," she said, forcing a smile as she hopped off the rock. "Because I'm going to need more than a little diversion once the efforts get underway. This party has been far more taxing than I thought it would be. Of course, that's probably because Aunt decided we should invite half the kingdom and a quarter of our neighboring states as well."

She put her gift, one of the cook's sweet berry biscuits wrapped in a cheesecloth, into the satchel. Then she carefully stowed the satchel beneath the rock.

"I need to go now," she said. "When I really do get into planning, the work is actually quite fun." Then she turned and made her way back up the sandy hill to the path.

CHAPTER
FIVE

R iver, if you—" River's father began.
      "I'm not going to let you fall!" River laughed. She gave her father's hand an extra tug. "We're walking in a straight line in the middle of the path! There's nothing for you to trip over!"

"Careful, Your Majesty," a young man called from the front of the crowd that followed them. "I wouldn't trust her." He gave River a smirk.

"Oh, you hush, Avery!" River called back.

River's aunt and the other courtiers and guests laughed. Even Stephan, from his usual place at her side, smiled.

The morning couldn't have been more perfect. Summer's direct rays had been replaced by the golden beams of autumn, and the leaves were just beginning to change from green to yellow. A delightful little breeze ruffled the long grasses on both sides of the path and made the boat moored at the dock bob up and down in the equally lively waters.

"It's my birthday, and what do I get for all my troubles?" the king cried. "A new hunting puppy like I asked? No. Not even a hearty breakfast. Just a 'Hello, Father. Here's a bowl of gruel. Now get dressed!' And now I'm being abducted as I starve, and my useless court sits by and cackles like a bunch of peckish hens."

The party laughed again as River and her father neared the dock. For all her teasing, River was being careful with how she led her blindfolded father. With every step, she checked to see that his foot was secure in its balsam wood shoe. That would be especially important as they made their way up the plank. In fact, she'd had the boat rails explicitly designed with this need in mind.

Taking her father on a boat for his birthday wasn't a decision she'd come to easily. Ever since receiving the special balsam slipper, her father had lived and thrived once again, growing strong and sturdy as he had been before. But there were limits to what one could do in a soft wooden shoe, rather than a boot, and the king had not always taken to his new limits well.

Going out upon the water was one such pursuit that had been denied him by his court and his daughter.

His daughter especially.

River had pleaded with him to stop his fishing trips, even after he was well again. "If the healer had left you another shoe," she'd reasoned, "I might not be so concerned. But you have no other shoe, and if you lose this one, I might lose you."

This conversation had oft been heavy in River's mind, even now, two years later. Before his accident, her father had loved taking the river down to the sea, fishing as he went.

So when she was gifted the opportunity to choose how the court would celebrate the king's birthday, she'd jumped. And after months of hard work, everything seemed to be falling into place.

"Now," she said, letting go of his hands and using his shoulders to push him into place. "Stand still and let me take the blindfold off."

"Oh, thank you," the king grumbled. "So kind of you." But she didn't miss the quirk of his mouth. He was enjoying this just as much as she was.

"Now," she said, removing the cloth. "Happy birthday!"

The king blinked in the brightness of the morning before his eyes focused on the boat before him. For a moment, he was silent, and the rest of the court behind him. Then he let out a shout. Whirling around, he grabbed River up in his arms and spun her around as he had when she was a little girl.

"You got me a boat!" he laughed. "My girl got me a boat!" Then he paused. "What is it about this boat that you'll let me sally forth in it where you wouldn't with all the others?"

River smiled and held out her hand. "I'll show you."

Eagerly, he took her hand, and she led him up the plank to where the captain and his men bowed.

"Captain Gregory," the king said with a nod. "I thank you for driving this fine vessel."

"It was all the princess's plan, Sire." The captain bowed back. "She made all the arrangements. All I have to do is let the vessel fly."

"If you look, Father," River said, pointing to the bottom of the railing, "I've had these railings made solid at the bottom. Instead of being wide open, there are holes to let extra water out rather than open metal railings. So if your shoe were to slip off, the water could be drained out, but your shoe couldn't."

"This," the king said, turning to the party that had followed them, "is why my daughter will be a better monarch than I one day."

The people let out a cheer, and River blushed as the king declared the party begun. Within minutes, music was playing from the other side of the boat where the musicians stood, and guests mingled with courtiers as servants ran around serving food and drink.

"You did well."

River looked up to see a young man sidle up beside her. His crisp military uniform showed off his impressively broad chest, the buttons glinting blindingly in the bright sun. They were silver, rather than gold, as he was a second son, but his uniform looked splendid nonetheless. He grabbed two goblets off the tray of a passing servant and handed one to River.

"Thank you, Avery." River took the drink with a triumphant smile. "He does seem happy, doesn't he?" She and the young prince watched as one of her cousins brought the king a present, a new fishing pole, which made her father chortle with delight. Then she turned her attention back to the prince.

"By the way, thank you for your most recent gift." She raised her glass. "I never told you my favorite color was purple."

His pale eyes glinted as he touched her sleeve. "It really isn't that hard to guess."

River laughed. "I guess not." She paused, then stood back. "I haven't seen you in ages. What have you been up to?"

Prince Avery ran his fingers through his thick honey-colored hair, which had been combed neatly to the side. "Oh, you know how it is. My father thinks we're not doing enough to keep up with your wheat production, so he's been pressing his farmers to use more of their land." He bumped her shoulder gently. "So I have you and your father to thank, I suppose, for my new load of labor disputes."

River snorted. "Serves you right."

Avery gasped. "Princess River. You don't mean to tell me you're planning to work me to the bone one day, too!"

River laughed, her heart leaping slightly in her chest. They'd never discussed their plans outright. Discussion had always been lighthearted and vague, and River wasn't even sure what the details were. But that they had plans... She liked that.

The day passed merrily. Bouts of dancing broke out from time to time when the music took the right turn. River's father swept her up into jigs and reels several times, and Prince Avery dared to pull her in for a few as well. The king's favorite cake was served with luncheon, alongside delicacies of crab cakes, caviar, and every kind of fish imaginable. And the king's joy was heard in another shout of adulation when River told him that the boat would be going all the way down the river and out to the sea by the end of the night.

Maybe, River thought as she watched her father with a smile, more responsibilities wouldn't be so bad. The party was obviously a success. She hadn't seen her father smile this much since her mother had died. Maybe she was more capable than she'd believed.

"River, come here."

River looked up to see her father gesturing to her. She went to his side, and he put a large arm around her shoulders and pulled her in against him. She nestled happily against his side, feeling safe and secure as she had when she was a little girl. The foreign dignitaries her father had been speaking with all bowed or curtsied.

A duke from a neighboring kingdom smiled. "When I saw her this morning, I said to myself, 'Surely this isn't the beautiful little Princess River! I feel as though she were only just in petticoats and stockings!'"

River blushed and smiled at the ground as the group laughed.

"She looks more like her mother every day," River's

father said, smiling down at her fondly. "And I couldn't be prouder."

River wished she could hold onto this feeling forever as the satisfaction in his voice warmed her chest like sunshine.

"Surely," a tall woman at the edge of the group said, "she is engaged to someone! She's too much in her bloom to be unspoken for!"

"I," the king said stoutly, "am in no hurry to marry my daughter off. Only the best of men shall suit her, and even then, none by my judgment. For I have promised River that she shall only be married when she's ready."

River grinned at her father as their guests gasped.

"That is quite...generous," one of the men finally spoke.

The king shrugged. "I'm healthy and well cared for." He gave his slippered foot a slight tap. "I see no reason to hurry her along for my own comfort." He gestured to a man across the deck, who had his arm around a pregnant woman. "John only just married, and he's older than I am. My child is competent and more than ready to take over the kingdom should she need to. There's no reason to tie her down before she is ready."

Dual waves of gratitude and guilt sloshed in River's stomach as he spoke these words. Her father believed her ready.

Was she?

"Besides," the king added in a mock whisper. "I don't think she'll need much help in that avenue." He gestured to Prince Avery, who was standing beside his father a little ways off. At that moment, Avery turned and caught River's eye. His smile widened with amusement when he recognized the focus of their attention, and River felt her cheeks warm as the king's guests nodded to themselves with knowing grins, seeming at ease once more.

"Will-o'-the-wisps!" someone cried. Everyone ran to the railing, and a gasp went up over the crowd as the water was suddenly covered with at least a dozen little blue whorls, their azure flames flickering over the water. It was dark enough that their incorporeal forms were easy to see. People immediately began to argue over whether or not the sight was a benign or malignant sign, but one of their sailors spotted a problem even more deadly than the little spirits of light.

"Look out!" he shouted. "Dead boat ahead!"

In the light of the wisps, River could just make out what he was pointing to. She would have missed it had the sailor not yelled. Another boat, a large fishing vessel, had run aground up ahead. Men that River could only assume to be the broken ship's crew, were still trying to make their way off the vessel and onto the bank.

"Brace for impact!" the captain shouted as he spun the wheel hard to the right.

River's father, Stephan, and Avery reached for River at the same time, but Avery and Stephan got to her first. Despite having two strong men bracing her against the impact, however, neither River nor anyone else was able to stay upright. The impact of the king's ship against the broken vessel was severe, wood and metal crunching in a terrible cacophony. River, Avery, Stephan, and everyone

around them hit the railing hard and the boat tilted danger-
ously to the side.

Screams and shouts filled the air as River reached up to
touch the throbbing place on her head. People around her
were crying as the captain barked orders.

"Are you well?"

River looked up to see Avery's face near hers, his blue
eyes wide as they searched hers. The nearness of him helped
bring her back to her senses.

"Father?" She grabbed Avery's arm and searched wildly
around her. "Where's my father?"

A strong pair of hands took her by her shoulders and
pulled her gently into a sitting position so she was at least
upright, though the ship was still at a tilt.

"Princess, are you hurt?" Stephan asked as he righted
her. His armor was dented in several places it hadn't been
before. He must have hit the ground hard.

"I'm fine!" River cried. "My father! Look for my
father!"

Stephan's face was grim, and Avery's face went from
confused to very white as he looked around them. Only then
did River realize that there weren't nearly as many people
on deck as there had been before.

With Stephan's assistance, she groped her way to where
the railing had been, only to realize that the collision had
smashed through it.. Her heart dropped into her stomach as
she peered over the jagged edge to realize just how many
people were in the water below.

Where was her father? River's heart sped so fast she

grew dizzy, and her chest was suddenly nearly too tight to breathe.

"Where is he?" she gasped.

"There," Stephan pointed to the shadows beneath the water. Twilight was nearly over, and the only light came from the bonfire the men on shore must have built. "See his guards? Kadlock and Walter are bringing him in."

River nearly fainted from relief as her father's body-guards hauled him up onto the sandy shore. More servants came running with blankets to warm him, and River was doubly grateful she'd insisted the king's personal physician attend the celebration as well. But even before her prayers of thanks could be fully worded in her heart, River's heart nearly stopped.

Her father's foot was bare.

"The shoe," she whispered to herself. Then she jumped to her feet as well as she could in her now-soaked party gown and turned to Stephan. "The shoe! Find the shoe! Everyone! Look in the water for the shoe!"

River's order spread faster than fire, and within moments, everyone, in and out of the water, was searching for the king's missing shoe. Sailors and guests jumped into the water to search as River stumbled down the gangplank to the riverbank to kneel at her father's side.

The king was pale and gasping as he lay weakly in the physician's arms. In response to the physician's questions, the king could only mumble and whimper.

It was a scene far too familiar for River to have any desire to relive it. She rose to her feet.

"Listen up!"

To her surprise, in the same way they usually did for her father, the chaotic court quieted the moment she opened her mouth. But this was no time to marvel.

"Whoever finds the king's slipper and brings it to us shall be rewarded!" She did her best to meet each guest's eyes. "A title, land, and riches. Whether you find it tonight or tomorrow or the next day, do not cease searching! And spread the word! Commoner or noble, I will make the reward worth the search!"

The ensuing chaos doubled as she turned and knelt back down beside her father.

"That's a lot to promise," Avery said in a low voice as River took her father's cold hand.

"And he is worth all of it." She clutched her father's hand as the sound of horses approached. "We'll find it, Father," she whispered. Then, nearly to herself, she added, "We will."

CHAPTER
SIX

Elliot sat back on his heels and ran his forearm over his face to wipe away the sweat trying to drip into his eyes. After staring morosely at the river, he glanced at all the other young men who were searching as well.

"No use looking in this place," one of his neighbors, a tall, fleshy young man, told his friend. "This part of the river has been searched to death for the last three days. If it was here, we'd have found it by now."

"Aye," his friend said, squinting in the sunlight. "My guess is that that slipper is long gone."

"I heard it was made of wood," the first man said as they rose to their feet. "Think something like that would float?"

"Who knows?" The other shrugged. "It was supposed to be made out of something special, but my cousin thinks that doctor was telling the king a tale. He says it was probably made of something out of the east..."

Elliot didn't listen to the rest of what the young man said. His large neighbor had a point. Supposedly, the king's slipper was made of balsam. That was wood, and wood floated. So why couldn't anyone find it?

As if to answer his own foolish question, Elliot looked left to where the channel met the sea.

That would be why.

News of the king's untimely birthday accident—and the princess's promised reward—had spread quickly throughout the land. King Oliver was beloved by most of his subjects, and that he should suffer yet another catastrophe by the hands of God was a topic of great discussion in the city. Elliot, like every other man in their little kingdom, had immediately joined in the search for the lost white slipper. That had been three days ago.

Much to Elliot's relief, his employer, Lord Gaskin, had been more than willing to allow him to join the search. It was his duty to his king, Lord Gaskin had said, to lend another set of hands to the search. Work had fallen by the wayside throughout the city in general as Elliot and all the other men had paused their own business to help the king.

There were some, of course, who boasted that their dedication had nothing to do with the princess's proclamation. It was all part of their loyal duty to the king, they cried.

Not Elliot. For as much fealty as he felt for his king, Elliot couldn't fool himself or anyone else about his motivations. He was doing this for the princess.

This bank of the river, however, seemed to care little for his motivation, noble or not. Like his neighbors before him, Elliot soon gave up and stood, his back and feet protesting as he moved out of his crouched position. He glanced to the left to see the place where he'd left the satchel before the insanity of the day had broken through. Hopefully, no one would be looking so hard that they found the satchel. The leather satchel had been the princess's, and Elliot wouldn't be able to replace it.

He was tempted to go and check it now. But no, that could wait. The king couldn't. Elliot sighed and made his way farther up the bank.

As the day wore on, those searching the bank grew fewer and fewer, just as they had for the last three days. A few fights broke out whenever something suspect floated to the top of the water or was discovered on the shore. But the object in question always turned out to be a large shell or, once, someone else's shoe that had fallen off in the mud and then washed down the stream.

But as hopes of land, riches, and title dwindled, so did the men's determination. One by one, they gave up and returned to the city. Not Elliot. Elliot scoured the banks and beaches, from the neck of the river to where it spilled into the sea. But by the eve of the third day, he had no more to show than any of the others. And his lamp was nearly out of oil. He had no choice but to return home.

Wet and tired, Elliot slogged back over the fields and through the town to his little cottage, his lamp sputtering with the remnants of his oil. The creak of the gate seemed unusually loud as he let himself in on the side of the big house, making Elliot cringe. If any family members had been asleep, they wouldn't be now.

Sure enough, one of the lower-level windows opened. Elliot froze where he was, suddenly aware of how he must look and smell. But to his relief, the face that peeked through was not that of his employer, but pale and wrinkled.

"Did you find it?" she called out, her pale eyes bright.

Elliot couldn't help smiling. "Unfortunately, no, Madam Balastrade." Then he paused. "I'm sorry if I woke you."

She waved a hand. "I only heard because I was listening for you." Then she leaned forward. "You're going out again tomorrow, aren't you?"

He gave her a sad smile. "I'm afraid I won't be able to. Your son was generous enough to give me three days, but today was the last."

Madam Balastrade scowled. "He can spare you another day. The king needs his shoe!"

"I haven't given up entirely," Elliot said slowly. "I just... need to find another way."

"Well, let me know when you do. I'm bored to tears in here." Her eyes gleamed mischievously in the low light of his lamp. "I might need a touch of rheumatism to cure that."

Elliot laughed and bowed. "Always at your service, madam."

The old woman winked and shut the window, and Elliot finished his trek to his little cottage.

His oil was completely gone by the time he unlocked his door, so he did his best to stumble through the darkness over to the fireplace, where he struggled for a moment to locate the flint he kept on the mantel. After several unsuccessful attempts, he finally struck a spark, and once the wood caught, he could see the inside of the cottage again.

There wasn't much to see. A thin bed beside the hearth with a small table and single stool on the other side. A shallow cupboard hung on the wall opposite the bed, and it was mostly empty, even by Elliot's standards. Half a loaf of bread, a few wild apples he'd picked up off the road, and a fist-sized slab of dried bacon that had mysteriously shown up on his doorstep the night before. At one time, he'd been mystified as to how food continued to show up on his doorstep, until he'd treated Madam Balastrade enough times to recognize the scent of her perfume on the kerchiefs the food often came wrapped in.

A soft thumping on the ground made Elliot look to his right. He smiled when he saw two shining eyes peeking out from behind his water jug.

"Hello, Sir Luke," Elliot said, bending to lift the little rabbit. He stroked the soft fur, enjoying how the creature's warmth felt against the rapidly cooling night. "I was wondering where you were. Here." He pulled a few leaves and wild carrots from his pocket and watched as the rabbit began to nibble them greedily. "I might not have found the king's slipper. But at least you got a good supper out of it."

After putting his rabbit down, Elliot stood again and stretched. No doubt about it, his cottage was small and cramped. But there *was* one corner of his room at which Elliot could gaze forever. Against the fourth wall stood a bookshelf that reached from floor to ceiling. It had been nearly impossible to fit through the door when he'd moved in, and Elliot could only credit his employer's desire to have a knowledgeable apothecary for the patience and servants it took to fit the thing through the door. Elliot had often hoped that the last three years he'd served Lord Gaskin had been thanks enough for the favor. Elliot was still employed, at any rate, so he supposed his work was at least acceptable. Either that, or his employer didn't want to bother with moving the bookshelf out again.

Now Elliot cut off a small slice of bacon and bread and sat on the stool, pondering the books on his shelf. Their leather bindings gleamed in the firelight. He'd read them all, of course. The collection was worth a fortune. His cousin had once callously suggested Elliot sell the collection and buy himself some clothes worth looking at. But then again, that was probably why Elliot's uncle had left the books to Elliot in the will, rather than to his son, Felix. The generosity and trust of that gesture had stunned Elliot and had added one more layer of tension to his relationship with his cousin.

Brushing the crumbs from his hands, then making sure they had no oily residue on them, Elliot stood and went to the shelf. Lightly, he ran his fingers across the books' leather bindings. With a sigh, he stopped at the fourth book in the second row and pulled it out. Why he did so, he wasn't sure. They weren't magical books in fabric or instruction. There would be nothing new left to learn that hadn't been there before. But he hadn't been lying when he'd told Madam Balastrade that he wasn't giving up.

He'd been reading several minutes when a bang at the door made him jump.

"Elliot!" a muffled voice called from the other side. "Your master told me you were in here. Let me in already. It's raining!"

Elliot sneered at the door but did as the voice bade. Better to have his cousin making a scene in his cottage rather than in Lord Gaskin's yard. At least in the little cottage, they could fight away from the eyes and ears of Elliot's employer.

When he opened the door, a burly man entered, shaking his arms and head so hard that droplets flew all over, many of them landing on the leather bindings of Elliot's precious books. Not that Felix would ever notice such things. Scowling, Elliot shut the door and grabbed a blanket from the bed to wipe his books dry.

"You really are as bad as he was," the man laughed, grabbing Elliot's only other blanket to dry his hair and face.

"What do you want, Felix?"

"I wanted to know if it's true."

Elliot rolled his eyes. "If what's true?"

"That you've been taking time off to search for the king's missing shoe."

Elliot folded the blanket carefully and returned it to the bed. "What is it to you if I have?"

Felix looked around at the cottage and shrugged. "Nothing. Just thought it was mighty presumptive of you to think you could ever deserve a princess's notice, even if you did find it. Awful bold of you to think she could ever need your help. Not that she'd remember you if she ever laid eyes on you more than once." Then he cackled to himself, as though he'd told a very good joke.

Elliot did his best not to let his anger or annoyance betray him. It had once been one of his aunt's favorite ways to goad him, telling other people that he looked like his mother, who was perfectly plain and forgettable in every way. He did, from what he remembered, favor his mother. But he'd always thought she was beautiful.

He'd also learned the hard way as a boy that rising to such insults was exactly what Felix wanted. And though Elliot was older than his cousin, there was no competition when it came to physical prowess. So he replied in an even tone.

"Lord Gaskin encouraged me to go, as he did most of his manservants. We were given three days to aid with the search." Elliot paused and couldn't help adding, "I saw you on the river, too. Yesterday, when you thought your fiancée wasn't looking."

Felix stopped laughing and his eyes darkened. "What of it? She'd like land and a title."

"I know she would." Elliot leveled a look at his cousin. "I also happen to know that she thinks you mix up your patients' remedies yourself. She boasts all about you in the square, you know, telling everyone about how brilliant you are." Elliot paused. "Has it ever occurred to you to tell her you purchase your salves and poultices?"

His cousin took a step toward Elliot, his fingers tightening into a fist. Elliot stared at him evenly. He'd felt that fist enough times not to fear it any longer.

"If you so much as breathe a word to her—" Felix began.

"Oh, I don't plan to." Elliot held up his hands, but he couldn't help smiling slightly. "I also don't plan to purchase my remedies anytime soon." He tapped his temple. "Because unlike you, I actually listened when your father taught. And I can make my own."

Felix stalked toward him until he had Elliot backed against the little table. Elliot knew better than to react badly to his cousin's taunts. That was a battle that he would never win. Not, at least, without vast amounts of training, something he wasn't likely to get anytime soon. But he held his cousin's searing gaze nevertheless.

"Stay away from my betrothed," Felix hissed. For a moment, Elliot thought he might strike, just for the pleasure of it. But after a moment, Felix backed up a step and spat on the floor. "And stay away from me."

"I would." Elliot said, straightening his shirt. "Except that you're in my house."

Felix looked around again, as if suddenly remembering where he was. Then he looked at Elliot once more before giving a strange laugh. "Yes, I suppose I am. It's too bad for you. This isn't anywhere I would ever ask a princess to stay."

Elliot kept his face calm as his cousin stomped back out into the rain, slamming the door behind him. But once Felix was gone, and the fire had crackled several times against the silence, Elliot felt his face and neck grow hot.

As much as it irked him, his cousin was right. Even if

Princess River knew who was sending her gifts, for he was sure she had no idea...even if she were willing to condescend to look upon him with the affection he liked to sometimes imagine, he could never imagine asking her to even deign to step into his little hovel. Daydreams and hidden notes and gifts could only take one so far.

But helping the king...

With a renewed energy, forgetting his long day of searching for the slipper, Elliot grabbed his book again, threw it open to the first page, and began to read.

CHAPTER
SEVEN

Y ou look tired," a deep voice said.

River gave a little jump.

"I'm sorry," Avery whispered, pressing a cup of tea into her hand. "I didn't mean to startle you."

River shook her head and bent her head appreciatively over the tea, inhaling deeply. It smelled of lemon, thyme, and one other flavor she couldn't make out. She took a sip and sighed. "Thank you. I didn't realize I needed that."

Avery frowned slightly. "It's been three weeks since the accident, and you've hardly slept more than four hours at a time."

River raised one brow. "And how do you know that?"

He gave her an equally wry smile. "Servants talk." Then he leaned forward. "I do wish you would stay in your own rooms, at least for a few nights. There are more than enough servants to look after him."

River looked back down at her father again and frowned.

He was dozing at the moment, but he could wake up at any time. He always did around this time in the afternoon. "I can't," she whispered. "He needs me here."

"Your father's advisers need you, too," the prince said, taking a sip of his own tea.

River sighed. "I met with them yesterday."

"That's the funny thing about a kingdom," Avery said with a shrug. "No matter how many times you tend to it, it seems to need tending again the next day."

River traced the rim of her cup with her finger. Her aunt decried the habit, saying it dirtied the cup. But today, she was too tired to care. "You know," she said slowly, "if you stayed with him, I would feel more comfortable meeting the advisers more often."

Avery's brow creased. "You know it doesn't really matter whether it's me or his valet or the physician's assistant. He can't tell who's there while he sleeps."

River looked down at her father's pale face and gently touched his hand. "I think he can."

Before Avery could argue, low voices sounded at the door, and after a moment, it was opened to reveal a young man. As soon as she saw him, River's heart plummeted.

It was the runner.

"What news do you carry?" Avery asked the runner as he bowed low. The young man, who could hardly be called more than a boy, looked briefly at Avery before returning his gaze to River.

"Your Highness," he said, bowing again. "You sent me out three weeks ago to find the doctor who made the shoe."

River nodded.

"He's dead, isn't he?" asked a rough voice.

Everyone turned to see the king's red eyes open and fixed upon the runner. The young man scrambled to bow low yet again, keeping his eyes on the ground as he rose and spoke. "He is, Sire."

The king let out a gusty sigh and nodded. "It was only to be expected. Couldn't get him to make second when he was here. And now the fool is gone, and I suppose I'm supposed to follow."

The room was silent as River, Avery, and the doctors and other attendants watched the king. At first, River wondered if he might rant as he sometimes did when he was feverish. Then she wondered if he might curl up and become unresponsive the way he often did when his pain was at its worst. Instead, however, she found his sharp gaze fixed on her and Avery.

"I'd like everyone to leave me," her father said, pushing himself up into a sitting position in the bed. "River, you stay."

River blinked at him as everyone did as the king wished. Avery offered a small smile and a nod as he, too, left the room. A moment later, she and her father were alone.

"Rest," he said softly, patting the edge of the bed. River, who had been sitting on a small stool beside the bed, was careful not to jostle the mattress when she leaned over. When she was finally settled, her head resting on the soft blanket, she heard herself release a sigh. He began to rub her hair the way he had when she was little, and she closed her eyes.

"You've been sleeping in here," he finally said.

River kept her eyes shut, but she nodded. He was silent for a while longer, then he spoke again.

"No one has come to help you?" His voice was so scratchy his words were difficult to understand, but River didn't care. For a moment, at least, he was thinking clearly. The king had returned. For the moment, she felt safe.

"Aunt has been helping the treasurer," River said slowly. "And Vonaparte has been very gracious in helping the cook organize and prepare the meals. Mistress Lonnie has been expertly organizing the servants, and General Thaden has been running the troops through their usual exercises."

The king watched her carefully for another moment before nodding again. "And Prince Avery," he said slowly. "How is he at quests?"

"I...I suppose he's quite good," River stuttered. "I've never seen him try." What was her father getting at?

To her surprise, the king simply nodded and patted her hand. "I'm sure he is. His father was quite ambitious in his own day..." He paused for a moment to adjust his position. But as he moved, he froze and then winced before panting slightly. "Call one of my lawyers. Make it...Jefferies. I have a declaration to make before their blasted soothing tea puts me to sleep again."

Nodding, River got up and did as he bid. What was he up to?

River and the rest of the palace had been terrified that

this second bout with his injury would make him as weak and helpless as it had the first time. To their relief, however, it hadn't. For while the physicians' healing tea did often put him to sleep, and he often woke in the night, moaning and pale, he had seemed less shocked by his pain this time, more resigned to what was and what needed to be.

After calling for Jeffries, River returned to his bedside, and studied her father. There was no feverish light in his eyes, no confused fog that sometimes filled them when he was in the most pain. Instead, there was a grim determination.

That determination was somewhat frightening.

"Father," River said slowly, "won't you tell me what you're doing?"

He turned and watched her for a long moment, his gaze haggard but sharp. "Do you really wish to know?"

"Of course."

He studied her a moment longer before giving her a sad smile. "You'll learn soon enough."

Usually, River knew what her father was planning. He'd taken special pains to include her in his rulings and deliberations over the past two years, making sure she understood why he was making this decision or that. They'd discussed judicial hearings and court debates, and River had been required to share her opinion with him so they might discuss it as he made his own judgments. He'd consulted her about taxes and aid rendered to the poor. They'd spent many a late night talking about their plans for the kingdom's future. This tight-lipped silence was new to her, and River decided as they waited that she didn't like it.

When Jefferies finally arrived, the king sat as tall as he could, though River could see just how much it pained him by the beads of sweat rolling down his temples. A few of the other lawyers bustled in as well, all holding quills, ink, parchments, and wax, and several of the courtiers followed as well. Avery loitered in the doorway, sending River an encouraging smile. River expected her father to chase the extra people out, as he'd summoned only Jefferies, but instead, he merely nodded to the others.

"I only called for one, but very well. You'll all hear what I say eventually. And word will get out faster this way."

"About what?" Avery mouthed to River.

She shrugged as her father turned to her.

"Daughter," he said with another sad smile. "Before we begin, I'm afraid that you're going to be very angry with me." He glanced at Avery, then back at her. "I never thought I would need to take these steps. But we are where we are." He paused, the soft light leaving his eyes and the grim determination returning. "You are my daughter," he said, his voice hardening slightly, "and I must also remind you that you're a princess first and foremost, and your duty is to your people."

"Of course, Father," she said, bowing her head. Really, such a reminder was almost insulting. Had he forgotten how she'd sat faithfully beside him every day for the last two years?

The king cleared his throat. "Let it be declared," he said,

his voice regaining something of its former strength, "that whatever man finds a method by which to replicate the lost balsam slipper or its effects shall have my kingdom as his own inheritance." He paused and glanced at River. "And my daughter's hand in marriage."

River stood and gaped at her father. Had he really just promised to give the kingdom...to give *her* to a complete stranger?

"Furthermore," the king continued, as though he hadn't just shattered River's world, "my successor, should someone complete the quest, will be the man who successfully performs the feat. Not his master or employer. Only the man himself."

A strange sound came from her right, and River turned to see Avery pale. Part of River's mind told her that this response in itself was troubling, but her head was still spinning too much to comprehend it.

For her entire life, River had been promised that she would marry only when she was ready, and only to the man they both deemed worthy. Once she'd come of marriageable age, she'd been the envy of her friends and the point of desire for many of the men. Heiress to the throne with the power to choose one's king made River arguably the most privileged woman in the realm.

Until now. Now, River was destined to marry whoever met the king's demands. Be he ancient, filthy, conniving, dumb, or cruel, he would be River's destiny.

Only a lifetime of training kept River from publicly demanding that the king explain himself. Whatever kind of father he was, as he had just reminded River, he was still king. Power might have been promised her, but that power was not yet hers.

It might never be now.

"Daughter?"

River realized everyone was looking at her.

"I'm sorry, Father," she said stiffly. "I didn't hear you."

"I asked if I have your agreement," her father said, gazing steadily at her.

River straightened. "As you wish, Father." And before her mouth could utter something truly disastrous or her stinging eyes betray her, River stormed out of the room.

"River!" Avery called after her. River kept walking, but he caught her easily. Placing his hands on her shoulders and forcing her to stop, he gave her a smile, though his face was still a shade grayer than usual. "He's out of his mind with pain," Avery said softly. "Once he feels better, we'll convince him to–"

"Did he look out of his mind to you?" River hissed. "Avery, that was a royal edict! They can't simply be revoked!" She shook her head and rubbed her temples. "He had a reason for that edict. I just wish I knew what it was."

Avery's face darkened. "And in the meantime, what if someone does replicate the effects of the shoe? What then?" He paused, and his eyes softened. "I thought we had plans."

"If you want to keep them," River snapped, "then you'd best get out of my palace and look!"

CHAPTER
EIGHT

"You're being unusually meticulous today," Madam Balastrade said, watching Elliot with wary eyes. "Even for you."

"I'm making sure your nerves are properly cared for," Elliot said, keeping his eyes on the cloth strip he was wrapping around the poultice he had set on the old woman's wrist. "Shaking hands aren't pleasant."

"You're trying not to think about a pretty face." The old woman smirked.

Giving her a begrudging smile, Elliot sat back and began to prepare a second poultice. One week had passed since he'd been able to search for the slipper. And without oil for his lamp, as he wouldn't be paid until the end of the month, he was reduced to reading in the light of the fire every night. But reading wouldn't help him find a slipper, and a thousand times each day, he imagined some obnoxious boy or lecherous old man discovering the slipper while he remained at Lord Gaskin's home to work. Or equally repulsive, an arrogant young man eager to catch the eye of any princess as long as she had gold.

Not, of course, as though the princess's reward would make him worthy of her attention. He would still be an orphaned peasant, even if he was as educated as many of the lower nobility. Dressing a donkey in the royal colors didn't make him equal to the task of pulling the royal carriage.

Elliot felt as though he might go mad.

"Well, if you're determined to stare at your work, I'll simply talk for you," Madam Balastrade continued. "Because you'll be interested to know that the king made a royal edict last night. The town criers announced it this morning."

"Oh?" Elliot said as he searched through his collection of herbs. Where was the sage?

"The king seems to have given up on finding the slipper," Madam Balastrade went on.

"And that deserved an edict?" Elliot chuckled.

Madam Balastrade poked him in the shoulder. "No, you distracted duck. The edict is that the first man who can recreate the slipper or replicate its effects shall inherit the throne and the princess's hand in marriage!"

Elliot had found his little satchel of sage, but at these words, his fingers seemed to stop working, and he dropped the whole thing upside-down.

"I thought that would get your attention." Madam

Balastrade grinned as she leaned back and watched him scoop up his spilled sage.

Elliot did his best to stuff the sage back into the satchel and continue with his ministrations, but it was suddenly all he could do to focus on the task at hand. Joy, fear, and determination now addled his brain. Thankfully, the poultices he was creating were simple and required little thought. A little lavender, and he was done. He had to try folding the poultice three times, however, before he could wrap it about her other wrist.

"I know you're dying to get back to those books of yours," Madam Balastrade laughed as Elliot fumbled to put the rest of his herbs back in their bag. "Go find the king's cure and marry his daughter. I do, however, expect to be invited to the palace for tea every now and then."

Elliot ran so fast that he nearly tripped on Sir Luke as he entered his little cottage. As he often did, he paused briefly to thank God that his employer was such a gracious man. For though Elliot was expected to create the salves, elixirs, tonics, poultices, and other general remedies that Lord Gaskin's large household might need, the rest of his time was free to spend as he chose. Often, this meant tending his herb garden, where he grew most of the herbs he used to create his medicines, or roaming the fields to search for rarer plants. But now, he had no such plans.

Feverishly, he picked up the nearest book and began reading. He'd read all two dozen of his books previously, of course. Multiple times. But never with such purpose.

Nothing had ever demanded so much of his books before. So Elliot continued to read.

Elliot read until he realized he needed to light a fire if he wished to see the words. The second time he looked up from his book was when he realized he'd given his supper to the rabbit and had eaten Sir Luke's carrots instead.

Finally, after he was forced to admit that his current book would do him no good, Elliot faced a crisis. Did he try to read every book he had? He could, of course. But by then, the king might be healed, or he might die. No, Elliot didn't have time to reread them all. He just had to choose the right one.

Standing, he went to the bookshelf and studied the bindings, which his uncle had carefully scratched the book names into with a little knife. Even without reading their titles, Elliot already knew what was in each book. At least, in general. His uncle had been very selective with the books he purchased. They could have been rich, Elliot's aunt had once complained, if his uncle would only stop buying books. Very few of the nobility even owned so many. Surely, there was something in Elliot's books' vast stores of knowledge that could help.

After staring at the books for several moments, though, Elliot decided to try another route. Carefully, he pulled a single piece of parchment from the thin stack he kept hidden beneath the books. His uncle had also left him the little pile of parchment when he died. There wasn't much left, so Elliot used it sparingly. But if ever there was a reason to use the paper, it was here and now.

Elliot dipped his quill in his little ink bottle and carefully made a list at the top, working hard to keep his handwriting as small and delicate as possible. More would fit on the page that way.

Possible Methods of Healing:
The medicinal properties of wood
Healing flowers
Sutures
Infection salves
Fae Potions

Not that he would ever be fool enough to deal with a fae potion. Using one of those on the princess's father was more likely to turn the poor king into one of those disturbingly bare cats than to actually help him. Elliot frowned and crossed that thought out. But as he looked back up to gaze at the twenty-four spines, he paused.

Most of his uncle's impressive book collection had centered around books about healing and medicinal preparation. But there was one book in the corner that he'd nearly forgotten he owned. Elliot had read it, of course, as he'd read all of them, but it was the least touched of all his books. Not only because it was a non-medicinal book, but also because it smelled of mold and was riddled with holes.

The Flora and Fauna of the Kingdoms of the Valley Chaisey

Elliot took the book down and began to leaf through it. A long time had passed since he'd read it, so long that he didn't remember most of what was in the book. His uncle had purchased it from a peddler, not because he was sure it would be very helpful, but more because the peddler was desperate to sell it, and his uncle could resist neither bargain nor books.

Now that Elliot examined it, though, he began to wonder with a palpitating heart if perhaps the book would be worth more than he'd ever believed. Because the more he thought about it, the more he remembered that the balsam the king's shoe was cut from had grown in a neighboring country, as had the physician. So flipping through, doing his best not to tear pages in his excitement, Elliot began to search.

There were dozens of little kingdoms in Chaisey Valley. It had all once been a vast empire, ruled by a dictator who had grown too greedy and stretched himself too far. But the kingdom in question, the physician's kingdom, was neighbor to Elliot's own country.

As he pored through the pages, frustration within Elliot began to build. He couldn't recall the name of the physician's kingdom. Only that he had come from the near east. But there had been many wars involving their eastern neighbors, and many of the old practices had been lost. And yet, if only—

There. One of the appendices was an illustrated map. Elliot set the book carefully down on the table and then stepped back to study it carefully. He had found the name of the physician's country. He was sure of it. The question was...had the balsam truly come from the same kingdom that the physician claimed as his own? And if so, was there a way to get some more of it?

Sending one last, exhausted gaze at the pile of books on his table, Elliot took this book instead and opened it. He was desperate enough to try anything.

CHAPTER
NINE

River carefully changed out the bandage on her father's foot, keeping her face hard despite the smell and fighting the urge to gag. The physician on call had run back to his quarters for some more herbs, and he had asked River to begin the bandage change without him. It wasn't a grand request, and until three days ago, she would have been happy to do it. She'd been changing his bandages for weeks.

But now...

"River," her father said.

River kept her eyes on her work.

"River, you can't ignore me forever."

Did he really want to bet on that? River very much doubted it. She could pretend to be mute for the remainder of her life if she so chose. And after the sampling of men who had come into the palace in the last three days, claiming to have cures, she just might.

"It's been three days," her father said. She could hear a frown seeping into his words. "Aren't we going to talk about this?"

Good. Let him frown.

"River, if you don't look at me now, I'm not going to tell you why I made the decree. And I haven't told any of our lawyers, so you can forget asking them."

River paused. He hadn't told any of their lawyers? She'd been planning to go to them this afternoon to ask, but if he hadn't told them...

Against her will, she lifted her eyes to meet her father's. A sheen of sweat covered his face, and his skin was unusually pale, even by recent standards. His eyes were red and glassy, and if she hadn't been so angry, her heart would have melted at his pain.

"Fine," she said, lifting her chin and leaning back on the stool. "Why did you promise to marry me off to the first stranger to waltz in with a cure?"

The king grimaced. "Riv—"

"Because I can see how that would benefit you quite well. But me on the other hand—"

"Would you stop talking and let me finish?" the king bellowed.

River shut her mouth, but she continued to glare.

The king ran a hand over his face and let out a gusty sigh. "I know it wasn't fair to you to tell you like that."

"You don't say." River crossed her arms.

"But there is a reason," he continued. Then he shook his head. "I know how you feel about Avery. I'm fond of him as well. I've watched him grow up, and his father is my closest friend."

River opened her mouth, but her father held his hand up, so she shut it again.

"But I'm afraid the boy isn't what his father hopes him to be," the king continued. "He's idle. And he's selfish. And before you argue with me, ask yourself this, daughter. I'm Avery's father's best friend. Exactly how much time or energy has he expended trying to save my life?"

River stared at her father. She wanted to rage and shout. She wanted to deny his charge vehemently. But now that she thought about it...

She couldn't.

"You make...impossible demands," she said. "Finding a cure or a new slip—"

"But did he even try?" the king asked gently.

As River made her way down the hall several minutes later, she still hadn't been able to think of a single way to prove her father wrong. And as the king's words echoed in her head, they were joined by a host of doubts she couldn't quell. So many doubts.

All these years, Avery had been leaving her little gifts. Poems and treats and pretty little baubles. But what else had he done?

As much as it pained her to admit it, her father was right. Half the kingdom was killing itself to find her father's cure, and Avery, aside from sending several knights out to join in the search, hadn't so much as set foot outside the palace.

As she was considering this, she nearly collided with Avery himself.

"Well, hello, my little thundercloud," he laughed, grabbing her shoulders to steady her. "I see you've been storming some more."

Usually, his teasing would have made River smile. But instead, she simply looked up into his eyes and tried to read them. What would he do if she told him of her inner struggles? Would he mock or make fun? Or would he take them seriously?

A bang from the palace entrance saved her from having to ask another question. She and Avery went down the hall to a parapet overlooking the entry as two guards below tried to fight back a tall, thin man.

"I need to speak with the king!" the young man shouted, his voice ringing through the stone halls. He was waving a piece of parchment in his right hand. "I can make a new shoe! I know how!"

"It's too late!" one of the guards growled, trying to hold him back. "Come back tomorrow!"

"But I need to see him tonight!" the young man cried. "I have the answer! I know how to find the wood!"

Avery made a scoffing sound, but River bent to examine the man more closely. He was young, though likely a few years older than she was. That, at least, placed him above half the applicants, who were nearly twice River's age. His clothes, while professional, were worn and patched in several places. His thick brown hair stuck up in every direction as he fought to get past the guards.

In spite of herself, River wished she could see him better. Something about this man intrigued her.

"What's all that din?" her father called out weakly from his room. Briefly forgetting her anger, River called back, "There's a young man here demanding to see you. He says he can make you a new shoe."

"What are you waiting for then?" the king cried. "Bring him in!"

"But, Sire," the king's steward said, appearing at the king's door and wrinkling his nose. "It's two hours until midnight! And he's half-mad!"

"Do you see any other young men trying to break down my door in hopes of healing me?" the king chuckled dryly. "Bring him in."

River wanted to remind her father that there had been a steady stream of young liars trying to break down his door. But as this young man was neither old nor hideous, nor did he smell like urine, she wanted to see what he had to say.

"But your Majesty–" Avery began.

"Is this kingdom yours or mine?" the king snapped. "I said bring him in!"

The young man was soon directed up the stairs. He was tall and thin with light brown hair and a surprisingly angular face. Avery glared at him as he passed, but the young man didn't even seem to notice the prince. His eyes were on River.

His steps didn't slow as he stared, and yet, his gaze was intense. Almost familiar. Incredibly impertinent, especially as he and River weren't acquainted. And yet...

There was something familiar about him. If only River could say what.

Unable to help her curiosity, she followed the young man and the guards who escorted him back to her father's chamber, where she stood in the doorway to see what this young man could do. It wasn't lost on her that if he was telling the truth, she might one day be his bride. And five minutes ago, that would have angered her very much. But after seeing his eyes...

No, she wouldn't imagine anything. She would simply wait and watch.

"Your Majesty," the young man said, bowing low. It seemed his manners hadn't escaped him completely, aside from trying to break down the palace doors in the middle of the night. "Thank you for seeing me at this hour."

"You've made a hefty promise," the king said, his sharp eyes moving up and down the young man's thin frame. "Tell me, what is your name?"

"Elliot, Sire."

The king frowned slightly, and River knew why. To omit one's tradename wasn't a choice that would endear him to the king's heart. Did he have something he wished to hide? A known rogue's name, perhaps? Or a dishonorable family?

Elliot, seeming to realize he'd made a mistake, hurried on, speaking quickly.

"I'm a...a shoemaker by trade, Sire."

Why did he hesitate? Did he think the king would scoff at a shoemaker?

"I see," said the king. "But the real question is, can you truly make the shoe?"

"I believe I can," Elliot spoke in a rush. "But... I'm a man of meager means. I have no horse, and the forest where the balsam grows is far from here. If I don't have a horse, it will take me far longer to get the wood that I need to make the shoe."

River's father leaned back into his pillows and studied the young man for a moment. Then his gaze flicked to River. She knew he was gauging her assessment. She kept her face impassive.

"What would a shoemaker know of finding a secret balsam?" he finally spoke again. "And why didn't you come forward sooner if the secret was really yours?"

"My uncle was an apothecary," Elliot replied. "He had little money for me, but he left me books. I've been searching the books, and just tonight, I came across a passage about a particular kind of balsam in the kingdom of Vashti that's said to have healing powers."

The king stilled at the mention of their neighboring kingdom, and River knew she had frozen as well.

"Vashti," Avery whispered over her shoulder, making River jump. Apparently, he had come into the king's chambers, too. "Isn't that the kingdom that physician—"

"Yes," River whispered back, her heart thumping unevenly in her chest. Was it true? Could this young man be speaking the truth?

"Do you have proof that what you say is true?" the king asked breathlessly. Elliot nodded and pulled a small,

tattered book from his worn cloak. He opened it to a particular page and came forward carefully to show the king.

River studied him again as he and the king spoke in
quiet tones over the book. What would it be like to be
married to such a man?

Neither his shoulders nor his chest were as impressive or
as wide as Avery's. Avery was a man of sport, hunting and
training with swords every day. But there was something...
gentle about this Elliot's spirit. River had never thought to
look to Avery for gentleness of spirit, and yet, it was there,
plain as day in this man's countenance. His deep brown eyes
were sharp and his gaze acute. River had felt its intensity
when he'd looked at her in the hall. And she couldn't shake
the strange feeling of familiarity that hit her when she'd
seen him first.

Where had she seen this man before?

"You see," Elliot was saying in a quiet voice, "this kind of
balsam wood grows only in this part of the forest. I'll need
to gather it and treat it before I can create the shoe."

"Where does it grow?" Avery boomed, striding forward.
"I want to see."

"Oh, no," the king said with a wry smile, snapping the
book shut before Avery could reach them. "That map is for
this young man's eyes only. But, of course, if you have a wish
to go and search for a cure on your own..." he let the words
trail off, but he held Avery's gaze until Avery took a step
back and nodded.

"Yes, Your Majesty," he murmured, then paused. "But
wouldn't it be better to have one of your own knights follow

this map to fetch the wood for you? Best not to risk wasting a royal horse on a beggar who's more like to run with it than–"

"Prince Avery!" River exclaimed, recalling that they were in public just in time to remember to use his title. Avery might be upset with her father's new terms, but that didn't give him a reason to be rude. If anything, Avery was making his plight worse in her father's eyes.

And hers as well.

Elliot looked furious enough that for a moment, River wondered if he might stomp over and strike the prince for the unjust accusation.

"No," River's father said, making everyone else look at him again. "No, I don't think I will. I think I'm going to loan this young man the horse he asks for." He sent Avery a warning glare. Then he turned back to Elliot.

"Now tell me, young man. Just how long do you think you'll need to make this shoe?"

The young man paused for a moment, his eyes darting to River before answering, "A fortnight," he finally said.

"Well," said River's father, "I'm going to be generous, and I'm going to give you not fourteen but fifteen days." He smiled slightly. "I'm aware that youth tend to be somewhat arrogant when it comes to what they're capable of in a particular period of time." Then the king's face hardened. "But know this. If you're in any way lying to me, you'll be judged a traitor and will forfeit your life for lying to the crown."

River wanted to interpose. Such a punishment was quite

harsh, particularly if he failed with good intentions. But there were too many people here to see.

The young man blanched slightly, but after a moment, he stood taller and drew in a deep breath. Then he nodded. "Yes, Sire."

Thin this man might be, but he was also brave.

"Get him some traveling supplies," the king said, waving at one of his servants. Then he paused. "Get him some new clothing, too. He can't go off looking for the king's cure looking like that."

"And give him something to eat," River heard herself saying. The young man, who had been gazing at her again, looked as though he might fall over from shock. At the last moment, he seemed to remember himself, and bowed.

"Thank you, P-Princess," he stuttered. "And Sire."

She gave him a hesitant smile before turning and making her way back down the hall.

Avery caught up with her before she'd gone three steps. "What do you think of him?" he asked, his tone derisive.

For some reason, something protective flared up in River's chest. Which was silly. She didn't even know the man.

"It's hard to know one's character in such a short time," she retorted.

Avery scoffed. "I'm amazed your father allowed him to pay you such insult."

River stopped walking. "What insult?"

"He stared at you like he was going to eat you."

This time, it was River who scoffed as she resumed walking. "You're seeing things."

"But truly," Avery continued, following her around a corner, "he had no right to look at you that way!"

"What way?"

"As if he knew you!"

River didn't respond. It was true, the young man had stared at her far more closely than was appropriate for one of her rank. But then again, she had the distinct feeling she did know him. Or at least, that she should know him.

"He wouldn't make much of a husband," Avery continued. "The wind could knock him over."

"Nothing some regular meals couldn't fix," River said in an even voice. His eyes. She should have gotten closer to see his eyes. Maybe she would have known them.

"And who carries a book—"

"When was the last time *you* read a book?" River halted and put her hands on her hips. "Because I haven't seen you pick one up in years. And don't tell me it's because you're too busy. I've seen you meander all around my palace since we were children, and I challenge you now to tell me where the library is."

Avery stared down at her for a long moment, shock apparent in his pale blue eyes. "River," he finally said, but she shook her head and started walking again.

"That's what I thought. And if you ask me," she continued, letting her voice grow in volume, "he was quite pleasing to the eyes! There was a brightness in them that showed courage! And determination!" They had reached the door to her rooms, and River stopped. "Things I haven't seen around *here* in a long time!" Then without pausing to hear his response, she flounced inside.

The servants shut the door behind her, but instead of moving into her bedchamber, where she'd intended to get dressed for the night, River let herself lean back against the door as tears pricked her eyes.

CHAPTER
TEN

Elliot felt conspicuous as he rode his borrowed horse home from the palace. He'd passed horses in the street every day and had never taken much notice of them. But now that he was on one, sitting high above everyone else's heads, he felt as though the world was watching him, despite it being the middle of the night.

They might as well be. He'd just promised the king that he could heal him. Elliot tried not to give in to the panic that suddenly threatened to take him, now that his initial burst of courage was spent and he'd said his piece in the palace.

Not that he regretted his gamble. Seeing the princess standing only feet away from him had hardened his determination. He had no guarantee of success. In reality, he could be chasing a dream, and the book his uncle had passed down to him might be full of someone's fanciful wishes. But Princess River...

Princess River was worth any risk.

The only regret Elliot did have was telling the king that he could complete the task in two weeks. He should have said three weeks. Or better yet, a month. But as Elliot had stood there with the princess's eyes fixed on him in the king's bedchamber, he'd felt desperate. After years of trading messages and gifts with her at their secret rock, he was suddenly sick of knowing that she knew him... but couldn't tell him from the next soul. So when the king had asked him how long the task would take, his frustration had come out, and he'd made a promise he was now doubting he could fulfill.

He also somewhat regretted lying to the king about his occupation. He wasn't a shoemaker. He'd never made a shoe in his life. But as the king had fixed his dark eyes upon him, Elliot had panicked. As it was, the king had been suspicious as to why Elliot had never come forward before. For while apothecaries weren't healers, exactly, they were close enough, and Elliot didn't want any more doubt cast upon his sudden appearance and promise of a cure.

That the prince from their northern neighboring kingdom had tried to get Elliot cast out of the palace had been bad enough. Elliot grimaced as he rode the horse to Lord Gaskin's stables and then walked around the back to his cottage. The thought of the sweet, passionate princess being married to such a lout was unimaginable. Rumor had it that they had meant to marry for a long time. And if Elliot didn't come through for the king...

Elliot shook his head to himself as he entered his

cottage. Sir Luke hopped up to him, so he picked his rabbit up and stroked him absently.

Sir Gaskin was always up early for his morning ride. Elliot would talk to him first thing and then set out immediately. Lord Gaskin would be reasonable, he'd been assured at the palace. He was a favorite with the king and wouldn't oppose someone in his employ attempting to heal their sovereign.

Setting Sir Luke down, he began to pack. There wasn't much to take. He had his two changes of clothes, one for church and his everyday clothes that he was wearing now. But thanks to the king, he now had a third set. Still, it would be better to take them all. Who knew what awaited him out on the road? Next, he placed his patched coat in the sack, along with several pairs of darned stockings. He was wearing his one pair of boots, and he had but two blankets, one to cover himself with in the case of rain, and one for sleeping. He would take his apothecary tools, of course, and his bottles of herbs and minerals. Those didn't take up much space. And the book with the map would remain hidden beneath his cloak. But his other books...

Where would he keep his books?

"Don't worry about those. You can leave them here for the time being."

Elliot whirled around to see Madam Balastrade standing in his doorway. He hurried to fetch her a stool. "Madam! It's late! You shouldn't be—"

She waved him off and slowly lowered himself onto his bed. "The king has already sent word to my son-in-law about your errand, offering compensation for your absence." She smiled. "The king is generous, and my son-in-law is more than ready to accept his generosity."

Elliot lowered the book he'd been holding. "Then I can leave them here?"

"Oh, yes. They'll be here when you get back." She fixed him with her sharp gaze. "Although, I shall be very disappointed if you don't win Princess River's heart and hand."

"I can't guarantee that I shall win either," Elliot said, his face suddenly hot. He put his book back on the shelf. "Word has it that she means to wed Prince Avery from up north."

The old woman *tsked*. "Why do you think the king offered her hand in marriage to the winner?"

Elliot froze. "You...you think—"

"I'm old, Elliot. Old enough to recognize what the king recognized. That young prince may be pretty to look at, but he wouldn't know a hard day's work if it hit him on the head. The princess, however..." She smiled.

"I'm only an apothecary," Elliot said quietly.

"If the princess is as kind and good as you say she is, then that won't matter." She poked Elliot's chest with her cane. "Now, your time to sleep is quickly running out, so I'm going back to my room to go to bed."

His chest suddenly tight, Elliot leaned forward and kissed the top of the old woman's head. "Thank you," he managed to croak out. "For everything."

She beamed at him. "If handsome young men kissed me every time I gave them good advice, I'd give out a lot more."

Then she chuckled as she rose slowly to her feet. Elliot rushed to assist her, but she waved him off. "I mean it. Save the king, and I don't think you'll have to worry about winning the princess."

"Why not?" he asked.

The old woman's eyes gleamed. "Because you'll already have won her."

E lliot set out before dawn the next morning. Lord Gaskin not only was pleased to send him on his quest, he even had the kitchens pack Elliot food for the journey as well. Then, using the map from his uncle's well-worn book, Elliot found the road and made his way east toward the place where the balsam wood supposedly grew. His heart beat erratically in his chest as he passed the palace and then even harder as he made his way out of the city.

He really was trying for the princess's hand.

"I never meant for things to go so far," he told the horse as they made their way down the dirt road. The sun was shining brightly, and the sky hadn't a cloud in it. Birds chirped quietly, and Sir Luke watched everything with his keen, large eyes from the opening in Elliot's bag.

Elliot generally tried not to think of his parents' deaths. That part of his life had been miserable and full of pain, young as he had been. Even now, it throbbed dully in his chest as he recalled the aching, hollow feeling of loss that had threatened to drown him when both of his parents had succumbed to the plague.

But even through the pain, Elliot had always been keenly aware of how much his parents loved one another.

His father had been an apothecary, and had helped his own father and brother in the family shop. Elliot's father's family had done well enough for themselves, well enough that when Elliot's father had fallen in love with his mother, whose family was quite poor, their marriage had been much frowned upon by Elliot's grandfather.

They hadn't owned much after the wedding. The bride's family couldn't afford many gifts, and the groom's family chose not to give them, a part of their protestation against the match. But the young couple had been happy. Elliot had never known a life of luxury, but he clearly remembered snuggles and hugs and kisses. He remembered being loved.

That had ended abruptly, however, with his parents' deaths. He'd gone to live with his uncle's family. His uncle was kind enough to him, but his aunt had been jealous. As Elliot was slightly older than Felix, his uncle's son, she'd worried that his uncle would use Elliot to replace Felix as heir to the family shop. And despite his uncle's protestations at such a scheme, his aunt had made it her mission to ensure that Elliot never grew too spoiled nor expected too much.

At the age of eight, Elliot had learned quickly that life could be far more lonely than he'd ever imagined.

Then, just when life had seemed its darkest, Elliot had seen *her*.

The princess and her father had made it a practice to go

out often to hand out food and blankets to the poor in the city streets.

Their first meeting was ingrained in his mind forever, like a smith making an imprint on metal. She was young, around his age, and her hair had been braided and coiled on her head like a crown, strewn with flowers as though some garden fairy had braided it. Her dress had been purple, and her hair had been even lighter back then than it was now. But her smile was still the same, one dimple on her right cheek. She'd flashed that smile at him when she spotted his pet rabbit. That was before Sir Luke. His first rabbit had been named Lady Marigold.

"Oh, what a lovely rabbit!" the princess had cried, running over and bending down in front of his rabbit. Then she'd turned her hazel eyes upon him. He'd never forget the way they sparkled. "Where did you get him?"

"Her," Elliot remembered answering in a daze. "Um, her name is Lady Marigold. And...um, I found her in my uncle's garden."

"She doesn't even try to run away from you!" the princess had giggled, holding her hand in front of his pet. Lady Marigold had sniffed her hand daintily, making the princess giggle more.

"She was a baby when I found her," Elliot had said, unable to tear his eyes from the little girl in front of him. "I taught her to stay near." Was this beautiful angel really talking to him?

"You did a good job," the princess had said, gently stroking the rabbit's ears. "She's very well-behaved."

As she'd continued to stroke his rabbit, Elliot had felt the first spark of hope since his parents had died months before. The home in which he now lived was one of tension and fear. Everyone seemed to tread on thin ice with one another. Someone was always fighting about something–usually his aunt–but this girl was like a sunbeam, chasing away the darkness. In that moment, Elliot had prayed he might see her again.

And he had. Whenever the princess and her father rode out into the city, she seemed to seek him out among the crowds where he waited, hoping to catch another glimpse of her. And to his surprise and delight, she always brought carrots for Lady Marigold and one of her brilliant smiles for him. He'd been so desperate to keep those smiles that when Lady Marigold had died, he'd gone hunting immediately for another rabbit.

The princess and the king had ceased going out into the city after the queen took ill and died. And for a long time, Elliot had been forced to admit that he would never talk to her again.

Their next encounter had happened much by accident. Well, it wasn't really an encounter, Elliot told himself. More a sighting. He'd been sent out to search for a particular herb for his uncle, when he'd spotted the princess standing on the riverbank, staring out over the water. Her face was streaked with tears, and he heard her call her mother's name over and over again, sobs beginning to rack her thin frame more with each cry. He'd nearly gone to her to offer her his handkerchief, the one his aunt insisted he keep clean and in his pocket in case he got dirty like a ruffian. But he'd checked himself just as he took the first step toward her. He was a poor orphan, and she was a princess. She probably had guards nearby to keep people like him away from her. So he'd forced his feet to carry him home with a heavy heart.

But he hadn't been able to sleep. He continued to see her beautiful, tear-streaked face whenever he closed his eyes. So the next time he could, he stole back to the riverbank where she had been. And he continued after that. Several times he went and saw no one. So many times that he nearly gave up. Her appearance at the river had to have been a one-time occurrence. But finally, to his astonishment, she was there again several weeks later.

This time, he didn't leave but waited until she left. Then he went to the rock where she'd been sitting both times, and he tried to think of something that might make her smile. He couldn't leave his rabbit, of course. But after a few minutes of thinking, he'd decided to gather as many wild-flowers as he could find. Then he'd carefully woven them into a little circlet and left them there on the rock.

A few days later, when he returned, there was a note of thanks waiting for him. He still had that note to this day, tucked into one of his favorite books for safekeeping. And with the note had been a piece of maple sugar candy.

So had begun their tradition of leaving gifts for one another. And though it stung more than a little that she had no idea who was leaving them, he'd always been encouraged that his gifts--humble as they were--could still make her smile.

As the years had passed, however, especially since he had come into manhood in his own right, it had bothered Elliot that he had nothing more to give than sundry trifles and little poems he thought up here and there. But what could a poor apothecary do? After his uncle died and Felix turned him out of the family shop, he'd barely managed to care for himself. What could he provide for a princess?

"This," he said to his horse as he climbed down. They had stopped at a stream, and he led his horse to the water for a drink. "I can do this."

The horse ignored him as it did the flies buzzing about, but Elliot took solace in his own words. For the first time in his life, he had the power to make the princess happy. Really happy. And he would do it if it killed him.

CHAPTER
ELEVEN

River put down the treaty she'd been reading and rubbed her eyes. She felt inexplicably restless. Well, not inexplicably. She knew exactly why she was restless. A week had passed since the shoemaker...Elliot had come to the palace. And though she knew not to expect him for at least another week, she couldn't seem to focus on anything else. Questions about him swirled continuously in her head like a maelstrom threatening to drown her in anxiety.

The week had not started well. The day after Elliot had appeared, she'd ventured down to the river to see if Avery had left her any gifts or messages. She doubted it after the way they'd parted last week. Neither had spoken to the other since. But still, she wondered if perhaps he'd left some token of peace.

But when she'd gotten to their rock, there was nothing new. He hadn't even taken the gift she'd left for him, an empty turtle shell she'd literally stumbled on while walking in the palace gardens several days before. Well, if he was going to be petty, that was his choice. She scooped up the turtle shell and returned it to her reticule with a huff.

Then, when she'd returned to the palace, she'd been given a simple one-line note informing her that Avery had gone off to search for the cure. No hint of affection or apology. Just letting her know.

Well, that was fine. River had work to do anyway. For the remainder of the week, she'd thrown herself into meetings and duties. But no matter how much work she took on, the worries continued to swirl.

First, of course, was the fear. What kind of man was this Elliot? He wasn't ancient, at least. One of River's greatest fears since her father's declaration was that some ancient healer would appear, and she would be forced to marry a man older than her father. Nor was he hideous. Not that she based a man's character on his looks, but she'd been telling the truth when telling Avery that Elliot was pleasing to the eyes. He wasn't as muscular or as tall as Avery, but as she'd pointed out, consistent meals could solve that. His brown eyes had been sharp and bright, and there was an honest openness to his face that she found herself wishing she could study more closely. His voice, while not distractingly deep, had a rich warmth to it. If sound could be like honey, his voice would embody the golden treat.

She hadn't touched his hands, of course, but she'd seen that one of them was bandaged, and she would hazard to guess that if she had felt them, they would be rough and calloused from his work. Cutting and shaping shoes all day had to do that.

What would it feel like for those hands to touch her? To have them caress her cheek or take her hand? Or pull her close as they danced?

Her heart did a strange little stumble, and she shook her head to clear it.

Unfortunately, his appearance was really of very little significance. More important was his character. After all, if he succeeded in his quest, he would be king one day.

And the father of her children.

River put a hand against her bedroom wall to steady herself as that thought flashed through her mind.

Her father might be convinced that whoever her future husband was, his ability to complete a quest signified his ability to rule. River wasn't convinced in the slightest.

"River?"

River startled slightly and turned to see her aunt watching her with delicately raised brows.

"Sorry, I didn't mean to scare you," her aunt said. "Beth let me in."

"Aunt!" River embraced her mother's sister. "I didn't know you were here! You were supposed to be on holiday this week!"

"Yes, I can tell," her aunt laughed, hugging her back. "Your father asked me to come and assist with some of the less enjoyable details of palace life, and your uncle had some business back in town, so we decided to finish our trip another time."

River let her aunt go but smiled up at her. "That would be absolutely wonderful."

But her aunt didn't smile back. Instead, she held River at arm's length and scrutinized her. "How are you?"

River forced a smile. "I'm just tired, that's all." She went to her desk and began absently sorting through the pile of parchments that had been stacked there.

"You've been good to your father," her aunt said as she carefully seated herself on one of the high-backed chairs across from the hearth. "Though I must admit, from what I hear, it seems as though you two aren't talking?" She paused. "Nor are you talking to Prince Avery, it would seem."

"I—" River began, but her aunt pressed on.

"And I have to wonder if perhaps this silence has to do with something...or someone else entirely."

"If the prince and my father wish to be petty and nonsensical," River answered icily, "they may do as they wish. I would simply request they not drag me along in their games." Against her will, her eyes began to prick. She had to blink several times before she could even read the parchment she held a handspan from her face.

"I didn't mean them," River's aunt said softly. "I meant *you.*"

River froze, then turned slowly to face her aunt. "Me?"

Her aunt gave her a small, sad smile. "You, my dear, are beloved by your people, and with good reason." She stood and went to River's balcony, opening it to the world below.

River followed slowly, unsure of what her aunt was about to do.

"But one day," her aunt said, looking out at the country-side below, "you won't be the sweet princess anymore. You'll be queen. And being queen involves hard things." She fixed her dark stare upon Eirin. "It involves protecting people. Sending men into battle. Doling out justice." She paused. "Being separated from the ones you love because you are above them. You must be."

River stared at her.

"I know life didn't turn out the way you'd hoped it would," her aunt said quietly. "It never does. But this is the position God Almighty purposed for *you*. And whether you feel ready or not, duty calls."

River had been prepared for a speech or lecture, but she suddenly found herself at a loss for words. All of the doubts and fears that had threatened to drown her for the last two years were now crashing down around her, and she felt as though they might soon swallow her up.

"All...the more reason not to marry me off," she managed to stutter. "Especially to some stranger just because he can procure a shoe."

She didn't say it aloud, but she couldn't help thinking.

All the better to marry her to someone she loved.

River had always wanted to rule beside her best friend. A companion. Someone with whom she could share all her fears and sorrows and dreams and joys. Someone she could trust with her kingdom, her children, and her heart.

"And you believe Avery is the one to do that?" her aunt asked gently.

"I do. I mean, I did." River looked down at the pile of parchments still in her hand.

There was one of the truths that had been bothering her the most. Not once had Avery ever offered to help with the daily tasks of running the kingdom. Her father's steward had offered his services incessantly. The head servants had fairly tripped over themselves to be of assistance. But Avery...

Avery had offered personal comfort. Food when she was hungry. A goblet of her favorite wine when she was anxious. Reminded her to sleep when she'd stayed up far too late looking over proposed laws. And when he had made the offers, she was touched. Really, though. How much had any of this aid cost *him*? The servants were the ones to prepare the food and fetch the wine. All he'd done was issue the orders to have them brought up. And reminding her to sleep? As thoughtful as it seemed, it required very little effort on his part.

What about the gifts? A small voice in her head wondered. Yes, the gifts had been lovely. But maybe they had simply helped fool her as well.

"But now?" her aunt prompted.

"It seems," River said slowly, "that Avery's not the kind of man I thought he was." Then she hurried to add, "Not that fulfilling a quest means the next stranger off the street will be that man either."

"Of course not," her aunt said gently. But her dark eyes watched River pace about her room with bright interest.

River felt a headache coming on.

Without thinking about what she was doing, she went to her bed. She knelt down and felt around beneath the bed until she found what she was looking for. Carefully, she pulled out a large wooden box.

"What is that?" her aunt asked, standing and coming over to join her.

Without answering, River opened the lid and stared at the contents inside. Five years of Avery's gifts. Many of them, the pretty leaves and flowers, had wilted, dried up, and fallen apart. But there was an assortment of pretty rocks, pinecones, a few ribbons, and a few lines of poetry written on scrap paper.

"What are all of these?" River's aunt laughed, picking up a sparkly rock. "Quite an assortment you have."

"The treasures of a child," River said, her voice constricting in her throat as she did. "But I'm not a child anymore."

River's aunt looked at her, and her gaze softened. "You're right. You're not." She looked back down. "Did you find all of this yourself?"

River was about to answer when something in the corner of the box caught her eye. She'd seen it before, of course. It was one of the poems. Actually, it wasn't the poem itself. It was the markings on the back of the poem. River lifted the paper carefully and turned it over in her hands.

Avery was many things, but economical wasn't one of

them. Paper was expensive for the layman. And this scrap, wherever it had come from, had been clipped from something else and used again. Avery would have never used paper a second time. Whoever left this poem, though...

For five years, whenever River had brought up the gifts, Avery had reacted with pleasure and humility. Several times, he had even asked her what she had liked about them. There was no way he could have confused this topic of conversation for another. She'd gushed about his thoughtfulness and described them in great detail.

There was no question about it. Even if he hadn't meant to do it in the beginning Avery had purposefully kept her believing that the gifts were his. And nearly six years was too long for that to be an accident. River closed the lid of the box with a snap, her face and neck hot.

"What's wrong?" her aunt asked, looking somewhat startled.

Instead of answering, River opened the door and motioned to Beth and the other ladies-in-waiting, who often waited in the next room over when River wanted to speak to her aunt in private. "Please cancel all of my appointments tomorrow," River told the girl. "I have something I need to do."

Beth bobbed a curtsey. "Yes, Your Highness."

"Oh...very well," her aunt said in confusion as River closed the door behind her. "Is it something I can help with?"

"No, thank you. This is something I need to do myself."

River was going to be queen someday. And her aunt was

right. Her life wasn't about her wishes or even her fears and anxieties. This was River's kingdom. And there were now holes in the fabric of what she'd believed the truth to be. She was still angry with her father, of course. Surprising her by giving her away in marriage was not what she needed right now. But she needed to push that anger to the back of her mind for the time being. These new questions were more pressing.

If only she could find a way to answer them.

CHAPTER
TWELVE

E lliot looked at the angle of the afternoon sun in exasperation. Seven days. It had taken him seven days to travel what should have taken four. He was already running out of time.

What had begun as a grand adventure had quickly become a journey of constant storms, monotony, and fae mischief, and only now had he reached his destination.

A violent storm had struck him on the second day. There had been so much lightning and hail that he'd been forced to seek shelter in a cave to save himself and his animals. By the time the storm let up, he'd lost a good half-day of travel. Another storm had struck the next day, and another the day after that. And when it wasn't raining, the roads became so muddy that he had to walk beside his horse to spare the poor creature as it trudged through the sucking, sticky mud.

The storms hadn't been his only delay. He'd awakened on the fifth morning to find himself in a fairy ring. The little red and purple mushrooms seemed to taunt him, keeping him stuck as his horse whinnied outside the ring with annoyance. This fairy hadn't made him dance, so that was something to be grateful for, he supposed. Still, it took him hours to figure out that he could wither the mushrooms by using a mix of three of the powders from his healing bag.

All in all, he'd wasted two and a half days on travel delays.

Still, according to the book's map, he had arrived. The forest loomed in front of him, and his pulse quickened. This was his chance to save the king, and in doing so, prove his affection to the girl who had stolen his heart so many years ago.

Elliot plunged into the forest, leading his horse behind him, and once they were sufficiently deep, let him wander nearby, happily munching on wild grass and flowers. He also let Sir Luke out of the bag, and the rabbit followed the horse's example, nibbling on the clover that grew in the shadow of the great trees.

The forest wasn't made of balsam, but this didn't surprise Elliot. According to his uncle's book, the trees of this forest were largely spruce trees. That particular brand of balsam he was seeking had been once fairy blessed, and long ago, had nearly been cut to extinction. There were very few left, which probably explained why the famous physician who had healed the king had refused to make him a second shoe.

Elliot wasn't exactly sure what he should be looking for. The trees around him were black spruce, a tree similar to those that grew near his home. They had dark, scaly bark, pointed needles, and the bulk of their branches was at the top of the tree. So, he decided quickly, his scheme was to search for a tree that... *wasn't* a spruce. The simplicity of his plan nagged at him, but it was the best he could think to do.

As he wandered through the forest now, he tried to think back to the time he'd seen a balsam tree as a child. Not the fairy-blessed kind he was seeking now, but a balsam tree nonetheless. His uncle had been asked by another apothecary to accompany him to a village downriver to examine a sick woman's wound. Felix had been too young to come along, so Elliot's uncle had brought him instead. Elliot couldn't remember much about the tree, but he still recalled its scent, which was similar to that of cinnamon mixed with earth and something stronger and slightly more pungent.

Elliot searched enthusiastically at first, marking his way as he went deeper into the forest. It wouldn't do to find the balsam, only to realize he was lost in the woods. By evening, however, his enthusiasm had waned, and he tied yet another torn strip of cloth around a tree with a sigh before deciding to make his bed there. He couldn't search through the night anyway.

"Well, Sir Luke," he said to his rabbit after making a fire," we're in a fine pickle. Even if we find the tree tomorrow, we've only eight days to return and fashion the shoe. But as the road is still muddy, I'm sure the journey back will also take more than four days. And as I've never made a shoe in my life, creating one to fit the king's foot comfortably will be a challenge for more than a day, I'll wager." He let out a heavy sigh and used a stick to stoke his fire.

Sir Luke looked at him with unsympathetic eyes, his pink nose twitching as he ate a dandelion.

"You're right," Elliot said, giving his rabbit a wry smile as the horse snuffed at Elliot's hair. "I guess there's nothing else to do but to get back to work in the morning." He laid down on the forest floor and wrapped himself in his blanket. Then he said a prayer of thanksgiving and desperation before quickly drifting off to sleep.

THIRTEEN

River woke up the next morning before dawn. Careful not to awaken her ladies-in-waiting, she dressed in one of her common dresses, smuggled an apple and a roll from the kitchens, and stole out of the palace just as the sun was about to rise.

The familiarity surrounding Elliot still niggled at River as she made her way through the palace gates and into the bustling streets. But try as she might, she couldn't remember where she could have seen him before. She wasn't familiar with any of the local shoemakers, which he had claimed to be.

What about someone posing as a commoner then, as she was doing now? She ran through her lists of local acquaintances in her head. She knew many of her father's lords, but Elliot definitely wasn't one of them, nor was he a member of a neighboring court. His clothes were respectable but worn, and he didn't have the air or confidence of a noble. A skilled tradesman then, as he had claimed.

Who was this man vying to win her people...and her heart?

Fortunately, River had more than a few knowledgeable contacts scattered throughout the city. And the woman she approached now was one of them.

Mallery, a rather plump woman and always red in the face, was selling her husband's vegetables in their stall at the northwest corner of the market, as she did every day. Mallery had a way of sizing people up that River had come to rely upon. She'd been invited to the palace on more than one occasion to quietly observe individuals making claims before the king, and more than once, River had rewarded her for sniffing out the scoundrels. Now, as River approached, she glanced up and smiled wryly.

"A sweet potato, Rachel?" she asked, her dark eyes glinting. Rachel was the name they'd agreed to use when River was posing as a commoner. For some reason, Mallery had always found it quite amusing to call the crown princess by her first, albeit wrong, name.

"Mallery," River said, nodding. "I would, thank you." She paid for the sweet potato. But as she counted out the coins, she pitched her voice low. "I'm looking for information on a young shoemaker by the name of Elliot."

Much to her chagrin, Mallery didn't smile knowingly the way she usually did. Instead, her brows furrowed as she took the money. "Shoemaker?" she asked, counting the coins slowly. "Never heard of a shoemaker by that name."

"Light brown hair. Average height and thin frame. Brown eyes?" River spoke quickly as other customers approached the stall.

Mallery frowned and shook her head, seeming ruffled at being flummoxed. "I'm sorry. We only have three shoemakers here, and I know them all. There aren't—"

"Not a shoemaker," Mallery's husband, Matthew, came to stand behind her. "But that sounds an awful lot like the apothecary two streets over. I knew him when we were boys." He paused. "At least, it did. Elliot was thin as a young man, but he got rather thick around the middle in his later years." He laughed and patted his own stomach.

Mallery's eyes cleared of their clouds, and she nodded quickly as Matthew went to see to the new customers. "Yes! That's the one!"

River frowned. "Then why would he say he was a shoemaker?" She paused. "And the man I'm referring to could only be a few years my senior."

Mallery pinched her lips slightly as she rearranged the potatoes in one of her baskets. "I can't answer that. But I would start there. Better than nothing, at least."

Mallery was right. At least it was a start.

"Thank you," River said, putting the sweet potato into the bag she'd brought with her. "Where did you say he lived?"

"Two streets down. The shop is called The Green Herb. It has a big sign and everything. You can't miss it."

After thanking the couple, River made her way two streets down and was relieved to easily locate the large sign.

She went inside and waited behind several other people until it was her turn to speak to the man behind the counter.

Much to her disappointment, however, the man had blue eyes and was above average height. And he definitely wasn't thin.

"How can I help you?" he asked in a booming voice. His blue eyes seemed to assess her as she assessed him. "Need healing tea? Boil powder? Chewing salts?"

"No, thank you," River said. "I'm looking for a man named Elliot."

The man stepped back and straightened. "I'm Felix. Elliot was my father. He died two years ago."

River blinked at him. "I'm...so sorry to hear that. I'm afraid there must be a mistake, though. I'm looking for a young man named Elliot."

The man stared at her for a moment before his eyes narrowed, and he gave her a rather unpleasant smile. "Must be my cousin you're looking for then."

"Your cousin?" River asked.

The man nodded and smiled smugly. "Named after my father. My parents took in the ungrateful brat after his parents died." He paused and tilted his head. "How'd a fine lady like you get to meet my cousin anyhow?"

River chose her words carefully. Giving herself away would be incredibly easy if she wasn't careful. Then her ruse would be shared all over the city, and she would have a much harder time blending into the crowds, not to mention merely escaping the palace.

"After the king declared that the first one to heal him should become heir to the throne, a young man named Elliot arrived at the palace. He claimed to be a shoemaker and said his uncle had left him a book detailing how he might find the wood to make the king a new slipper like the one he lost."

The man looked her up and down again, frowning slightly. "You work for the king then?"

She allowed herself a wry grin. "Yes, I do." This wasn't a lie.

The man seemed to war with himself for a moment before huffing and looking at the door, all signs of welcome gone. "Well, for one thing, my cousin was lying to His Majesty. He's not a shoemaker."

River felt her stomach drop, but she kept her face impassive. It was a skill she'd come to excel at in recent years. "Oh?" she asked evenly.

"He's an apothecary. Instead of joining the family trade like the rest of us, though, he took up a job with Lord Gaskin."

Finally, River thought. A name she knew.

"He lives in a cottage on the lord's town property." Felix jerked his thumb to his right. "Up on that fancy street just outside the palace walls. Only house on the street with a blue door."

"And your cousin lives with Lord Gaskin's family, then?" River asked.

"Yes. His Grace's wife has delicate health and doesn't wish to leave her family in the city. So instead of moving back and forth between the city and the country like most of them nobles do, they stay here in town all year." He leaned over the wooden counter. "But if you want to serve your king, take my advice. Stay away from Elliot. Better yet, have him arrested. Lying to the king and all. It doesn't really surprise me, though for the life of me, I can't understand why he called himself a shoemaker." Felix snorted then muttered under his breath, "Always was an odd one."

River left the apothecary with more questions than she'd come with, and she regretted eating the apple and roll, as her stomach was now doing an excellent job of tying itself into knots.

Not only had the young man lied about his occupation, but his own family didn't even approve of him. Who in the world was her father forcing her to marry? Lying to the crown was punishable by death. Being an apothecary was a respectable trade, and a more revered position than that of a shoemaker.

And she still hadn't the slightest clue why he looked so familiar.

More determined than ever, River made her way back up to the wealthier side of town. From what she knew, the apothecary had spoken the truth. Lord Gaskin, of course, had his own land out in the country. All of the nobility did. But many, including Lord Gaskin, also kept a home in town for when the king wished for them to be near. And from the latest gossip, he had ceased going back and forth between town and country due to his wife's frail health.

The house wasn't hard to find. The wealthiest people in

the city lived in the mansions along the street that bordered the palace walls. And as Felix had predicted, it was the only house on the street with a blue door.

A servant answered her knock.

"Good morning," River said pleasantly. "I need to speak with Lord Gaskin."

"His Grace doesn't see commoners off the street." The servant, a thin woman, scowled. "Make an appointment with his scribe in the office in the city." She began to shut the door in River's face, but River put her hand out and held the door open.

"I'm here in the name of the king," she said, holding out the signet ring she wore. The woman scowled, but after examining the ring, her eyes flew open wide, and she threw the door open wide and gestured for River to come inside.

"My apologies, Miss!" she said, hurrying to shut the door behind River. "It's just that we don't usually get the king's messengers this way. They usually go to His Grace's office in the city."

"I see," River said. "Well, I'm here now, and I'd like to speak with His Grace. It's a matter of urgency."

The woman paled slightly. "I'm so sorry, Miss," she said, glancing up at the top of the circular banister. "He's out to the palace this morning." She paused and frowned. "Per-haps you could see Lady–"

"Nonsense, Ritah." An old woman with piercing blue eyes emerged from one of the back rooms. "Leave my daughter be. She's not feeling well today." The old woman was rather plump, and she walked slowly, as if it pained her, but her gaze was sharp. "Perhaps I can be of assistance. I'm Lord Gaskin's mother-in-law."

"Thank you, madam," River said. "I'm looking for information on a young man named Elliot."

To River's surprise, the woman's eyes lit up. "I see," she said. She waved a hand at the servant. "Fetch some tea and refreshments for myself and our guest. Serve them up in the blue room."

"Yes, Madam Balastrade," the servant said, scurrying in the other direction.

"Sorry for Ritah," the old woman said as they moved into a small but well-furnished parlor. "Usually, Travis, our butler, greets our guests. Unfortunately, he's ill today, and we're a bit short-staffed." She slowly seated herself on a blue cushioned chair and indicated the door. "Would you mind closing that? I'm supposing you don't want the entire staff to hear the king's business. Then you can sit here."

River hurried to close the door then sat in the seat the old woman pointed to.

"Now," the old woman said pleasantly as she leaned back into the chair. "What can I do for you, Your Highness?"

River blanched at her. "How...Pardon me, but how did you know?"

"Fah!" The old woman laughed. "I was in the palace with my daughter the day you were born, and have been there many times since. You think I wouldn't know my princess?"

River flushed slightly. "I'm sorry for the deception."

The old woman's eyes only sparkled. "I think better of

you for it. More rulers should go out among their people every now and then. It would keep them a little more humble."

River flushed again at the praise. "You said you can help me learn about Elliot?"

"I can." The old woman paused. "But if I may be so bold, what are your intentions when it comes to our apothecary?"

River swallowed. "I'm...not sure, I suppose. I came to learn more about him after he appeared in my father's court." She paused. "My intention is to find the truth. I want to know who wishes to claim my kingdom as his own."

Madam Balastrade raised one white brow. "And, I'm guessing, your hand?"

Her face hot, River nodded. "I tracked him to his cousin's apothecary shop, where I was told that he lied to the crown."

"Lied?" The old woman's white eyebrows shot up. "How so?"

"He said he was a shoemaker," River said hesitantly. She was surprised then when the old woman let out a laugh.

"He did, did he?"

River couldn't see what was so funny. Lying to the king was a crime, and while River was quite annoyed with the young man, she didn't want him to be put to death. "Why do you think he said such a thing?" she asked.

"I haven't the slightest idea. Come in, Ritah."

River hadn't heard a knock at the door, but the old woman's hearing must have been exceptional because the door opened, and Ritah entered carrying platters of tea and small cakes. Once the tea was served and the food spread out, she scurried out, closing the door firmly behind her.

"As I said," the old woman continued, pouring River a cup of tea, "I don't know why he said that. Possibly to keep from being laughed out of the court, being an apothecary promising to make a shoe and all. And yes, I did hear about that."

River couldn't help but remember how the young man had been mocked upon arriving. The old woman did have a point.

"But," Madam Balastrade continued, "I can tell you that your father's health couldn't be in better hands."

"How so?" River asked.

"He's incredibly skilled. While his witch of an aunt made sure he knew his place in his uncle's house—that would be Felix's mother and father—his uncle taught him everything he knew. Left him his books, too."

That would make sense. River remembered noting upon seeing Elliot's book how incredibly rare it was for a commoner, even a skilled worker, to own one.

"I'm guessing you talked to Felix," the old woman continued, this time pouring her own tea. "Felix is a pompous bully who purchases his herbs from other apothecaries because he didn't apply himself to learning what his father had to teach." Madam Balastrade's eyes gleamed. "But Elliot did."

River suddenly felt restless, as though she'd been sitting for hours, rather than just a few minutes. "Do you...do you think he'll be successful?"

Madam Balastrade studied her for a moment before slowly getting to her feet. River tried to help her, but she just waved River away.

"It's good for this old body to do some work every now and then. All right, follow me."

River followed, slowing her pace to match the old woman's. Where was she taking her? When she'd left the palace this morning, she hadn't imagined her day would be this complicated at all.

They made their way out one of the back doors to a large garden. In the middle of the garden was a tiny cottage. Madam Balastrade reached into a hole in the door's wooden beam and pulled out a large brass key. Then she fit the key into the door of the little wooden cottage. The lock clicked, and the door swung open. Madam Balastrade waved for River to follow.

"This is where he lives?" River asked as the old woman closed the door behind them. The cottage had been white-washed on the outside, but the inside was dark. If it hadn't been for the two glass windows, seeing would have been nearly impossible. A hearth lay dark on the south side of the room. The furniture was sparse and bare. There was a bed beneath the window, and a plain table with two stools. And then River turned around.

"How in the...so many books!" she exclaimed.

Owning one book was something most commoners could never even dream of. But this young man owned eleven. Twelve, if he'd taken the tattered book with him on the journey. River went to the bookshelf and brushed several of the spines with her fingertips.

They were real.

Then her manners got the best of her. "These are his personal quarters," she said, turning to the old woman. "I feel as if I'm trespassing."

"He would nearly die of elation if he knew you were in here." Madam Balastrade smiled. Then she handed River the key. "I'm going to go sit on the bench outside and rest my legs. Look around. Draw what conclusions you will." Then she left.

As she looked around, River was struck by the sensation that Lord Gaskin was a rather cheap man. He was one of the wealthiest lords in the court, a fact he liked to flaunt subtly at balls and other grand gatherings. And while the cottage did have real glass windows, Lord Gaskin seemed to have furnished the room to be as meager as Elliot's meals probably were, judging by the size of the little cupboard on the wall. It couldn't possibly hold more than a loaf of bread and a few fruits and vegetables at the most.

If Elliot could afford to fill it.

The mattress on the bed was threadbare, and everything personal seemed to have been stripped from the room. There really weren't many conclusions to draw. He was poor but quite educated. He seemed to be kind to Lord Gaskin's mother-in-law, based on how fond she seemed of him, and he'd had a row of some sort with his family. But just as River was ready to leave, a slip of parchment on the floor caught her eye.

She bent to pick it up and examined the small scrap. One side had words scribbled on it. For some reason, this looked familiar as well, though River had so many questions swirling around in her head that she couldn't remember why. The scrap had obviously been cut from a larger piece of paper, as the words were all cut off and made no sense by themselves. When she turned it over, however...

There was a sketch of a rabbit. It had floppy ears, and though the picture had no color, the hand that had drawn it had been skilled enough to make it look as though it were brown.

To her dismay and intrigue, this rabbit, like Elliot, looked familiar.

But the rabbit wasn't alone. Beside it knelt a girl in a fine dress, her hair coiled in a braid like a crown on her head. She was smiling at the rabbit, and her left hand was buried deep in its soft fur.

Another foggy memory, like a small flame, struggled at first, then burst into light in her mind. She flipped the paper over again and examined the handwriting, then she gasped. When she heard the door creak, she looked up to find the old woman standing in the doorway again. Unable to put her thoughts into words, River merely held up the drawing as though it would explain everything.

Madam Balastrade just smiled.

CHAPTER
FOURTEEN

Doubt had been River's constant companion since her mother died. Fear that she could never fill her mother's shoes. That she would disappoint her father. That she would fail her kingdom.

But as she strode up to the palace, River felt as though she were returning a different person than she'd been when setting out that morning. For when she'd snuck out, River had still been a girl. But now she threw her hood back, making the guards gape and hasten bows, her head high and her back straight.

It was time for River to be a woman.

More of her servants gasped and hurried to open doors as she entered the palace. If they were scandalized by her common attire, none were brave enough to admit to it, which was a good thing. River was in no mood for foolishness. She would have enough of that to deal with tonight.

"Your Highness!" her father's steward hurried to catch

up with her as she strode through the main hall. "No one knew where you were. We were quite worried!"

"Thank you for your concern." She slowed to give him a smile, then resumed her quick step. "Is Prince Avery still gone?"

"No, Your Highness. He returned this morning."

Of course, he did. River nearly rolled her eyes. The man couldn't even spend a whole week seeking her father's cure or her hand in marriage. Then whose castle did he return to in his failure?

Not his own.

Now that she thought about it, she wondered how long he had been visiting. Not that it mattered. She knew now what kind of man he really was.

"Prepare a feast for tonight. Invite him, but no one else. I want minimum staffing, just enough to serve dinner. And..." She paused. "Please choose with discretion." She gave him a meaningful nod.

The steward blinked at her before nodding back. "Of course, Your Highness."

"I'm going to change." She stopped at the foot of the stairs. "Please have my mother's coronation jewels brought to my chambers." She paused. "And her crown."

When she looked at him, the steward's eyes looked wide enough to fall out of his head. But then they began to sparkle, and he smiled as he bowed. "Yes, Your Highness."

Was it just River, or had his address sounded far more reverent than usual?

River's ladies-in-waiting were all in a tizzy when she

returned, fussing over her common clothing and begging to be told where she had gone. Instead of answering their questions, however, she simply smiled and shook her head.

"You'll all know in good time. But for now, I wish for my best gown. My mother's jewels will be arriving any moment, and I need to be ready for this evening."

This caused an even greater stir, but when River's aunt stepped in and saw what was happening, she scolded the girls for being so silly. This set them to work, brushing and pinning River's hair, dressing her in the magnificent gown of purple silk, and applying the appropriate color to her lips and cheeks. Then River's aunt took the jewels from the servant who brought them, and when River was ready, she placed them on River herself.

"I've been waiting to do this for years," she whispered, lowering the crown gently on River's brow.

River stared back at the woman in the mirror. The jawline, nose, and chin she knew. But the woman's eyes...

They were hard and determined, not timid or afraid anymore. She sat erect rather than hunched over, and though the crown was delicate and feminine, it gave her the sense of power she'd always feared would elude her. Then she turned to face her aunt. "You don't think Father will—"

"Your father has wanted you to take this crown for years." Her aunt grinned. "And your mother..." Her voice caught, and she had to clear her throat twice before speaking again. "Your Mother's greatest regret was that she would never see you wear it."

Dinner was announced soon after that, and when River

arrived at the dining hall, it was clear of everyone but the necessary servants and Avery, just as she had ordered. He had been reclining in a chair near the hearth, but when she entered, he quickly stood and approached her. As he neared, however, he stopped, and his eyes widened.

"You, my darling, look like a queen," he said in a reverent voice.

"Thank you," she said with a nod. And for a moment... just a moment, she wondered if he might be capable of changing, too. But then the boyish grin returned, and he tried to catch her around the waist. River caught his hand instead and tucked her arm beneath his. He scowled slightly, but then his easy smile returned.

"I wish you'd dress this way for all our events. The other men wouldn't be able to take their eyes off you."

Once again, River had to work to keep her face impassive. Had he always been this way before? Shallow and ill-focused? Or was it a new development brought on by her new persona?

"How did your search go?" she asked as he pulled out her chair. "Did you find anything?"

His grin vanished briefly before appearing again. "It was, unfortunately, unsuccessful. But," he said, holding up a finger, "I've left men to continue the search for me."

"You know my father's edict stipulated that the one to marry me would have to be the one to find it," River said.

Avery shrugged, but his brow furrowed slightly. "I'm going back out tomorrow."

"You know," River said, her voice still nonchalant, "If

one of your men found it, I would have to marry him instead."

Avery's jaw tightened, but he refrained from answering as the servants brought the first course.

"Where did you look?" River asked.

"Over near that forest, the one the shoemaker mentioned." His mouth quirked up in a smile.

River tensed. "What's so funny?"

"Oh, nothing." He waved her off. But River put down her fork.

"Avery, if you don't–"

Avery rolled his eyes. "I swear, River. Sometimes you're the biggest fuddy-duddy. No need to get excited. I knew you wouldn't be satisfied with the outcome of your father's edict, so before I left, I paid a fairy to find the shoemaker and put him in a fairy ring. And possibly to send a few bouts of nasty weather. Nothing so bad. I'm told he already escaped, and it gave me a few days to catch up."

River had begun to take her first bite, but at these words, she dropped her fork, which hit her plate with a crash. "You did *what*?"

He snorted. "I thought you'd be impressed."

"Impressed that you cheated? Or that you put the man in danger?"

Avery huffed and tossed his own silverware down. "What do you want from me, River? You wanted me to go searching. I did. You wanted to get married. I saved you from marriage to a total stranger. You–"

River held up a hand. For a long moment, the silence

roared in her ears as she attempted to keep control of her temper. She couldn't lose it now.

"Let's talk about something else," she finally said, picking up her utensils again. "Have you recently visited the bend in the river?"

He laughed a little, though it was strained. "Which one? You'll have to be more specific."

Just as River had thought. And yet, she played along. If he wanted to pretend, so could she.

"The one with the large, flat rock." She made her voice sugary sweet. "The one we've been exchanging presents at for the last five and a half years." She paused. "What did you think of the present I left? Did you like it?" She put on an excited, adoring look of girlish hope and delight.

He stared at her for a long moment before grinning and nodding. "Of course. It was lovely. Whatever made you think of it?"

But instead of answering, she simply stared at him, letting the girlish grin slip away. And after several long moments, he looked down at his plate.

As insane as her father's edict was, he had been wise enough to see that this young man should never sit on his throne. And River was only too grateful to see it now, too.

Especially on this side of the wedding.

"Everyone out," she boomed. The servants, who must have been warned ahead of time, scurried to leave. Half a minute later, they were completely alone. Avery watched her with wide eyes.

Finally, she began to eat again. "Tell me," she said, doing

her best to sound conversational, "if you were to marry me today and become king, what would your first edict be?"

Relief filled Avery's face, and he relaxed slightly. "I would have an entirely new wardrobe commissioned for you," he said. "With the exception of that magnificent gown, of course, your dresses have gotten a little out of mode, and your father never pays attention to such things."

River blinked. That had...not been the answer she'd expected.

"And..." she said, "your father pays attention to your sister's wardrobe?"

"Well, no—"

"Does your older brother?"

Annoyance flashed across his face. "No, but a queen ought to look above the rest." His gaze softened. "And you deserve the best, you know."

"What about my people?" she asked. "What would you do for them?" Surely, his father hadn't neglected to teach him civics. He might be a second-born prince, but if something ever happened to his brother, he'd be next.

How had she not thought to ask him these things before?

"Hm," he said, chewing slowly. "That's a good question. I think...I think your father is losing extra revenue. I would seek to remedy that."

Well, that answer wasn't completely buffoonish. Maybe there was hope. "How so?" she asked.

"By keeping your taxes so low."

She frowned. "Do tell."

"Well, your father showed me some of your revenue numbers recently, and your farmers take home quite a large margin of what they make. Your father's charges to them are minimal at best."

"So you—"

"And your tradesmen keep even more than the farmers." He paused, then his blue eyes gleamed. "Not that that would be something to figure out immediately. We would have lots of time to discuss such matters after we had time to...enjoy being married."

River barely stuffed down the urge to throw a piece of her bread at his head. Instead, she stood and forced a smile. "Thank you for your time, Prince Avery. You've told me everything I need to know." Then she turned and made her way to the door. When she neared the doors, the sudden scurry of servants she could hear on the other side made it clear they'd been listening at the keyhole. They were still scattering when the doors were opened for her and she walked through. Once they were closed, she stopped.

"Mistress Irene," she said, rounding on the head housekeeper. Mistress Irene was quite pale, and her voice faltered slightly.

"Y–yes, Your Highness?"

But she needn't have worried. River gave her a wry grin. "Tell Franc that dinner was excellent."

After a moment, Mistress Irene's face regained its color, and she grinned, too. "Of course, Your Highness." Then with a bobbed curtsey, she shooed the others away.

"That was expertly done, Your Highness," the steward

murmured, joining her as she made her way to her room. "If I'm to be so bold."

She smiled at him, but suddenly felt unusually tired. "Thank you. Your opinion is one I hold in high regard, so I'm glad you approve."

After inquiring about her father's health, she retired to her own chambers, exhausted and somewhat shaky.

Today, she had put off the princess and put on the queen. But the matter of her marriage still wasn't final. While she was rather certain she knew who this Elliot was and why he looked so familiar, she couldn't know for certain until they spoke again. And he had only a week to reappear.

But this was no time for misgivings, uncertain as her circumstances may be. She was no longer the frightened little princess. She couldn't be. She had been placed, as her aunt had reminded her, here in this position now. This was her burden to bear.

Her duty.

She'd been running from it for a long time. Since her mother's death, really. But now, she must rise to it.

She took off the crown and set it on her vanity, watching as the gems caught her fire's weak light and sent it soaring up onto the ceiling in thin bursts of violet.

She could rise to her place in the world, God willing. She just hoped her heart could rise to the challenge as well.

CHAPTER
FIFTEEN

Elliot woke up and immediately wished he could go back to sleep. It had rained again that night, and in spite of his makeshift tent, which consisted of one of his blankets stretched over several branches, he was soaked.

It was also his tenth day. The last day he could search, travel home, and create anything that somewhat resembled a shoe.

He ate a little breakfast and then began trudging through the forest once more. The day was warm enough that his clothes eventually dried, but this did little to lighten his heart.

What a fool he had been for hoping to win the princess. When he'd set out on this journey, it had all seemed a great adventure, something like the stories his mother had told him when he was small. But reality wasn't a story. Just as the rain had soaked him through and through, so had the truth.

What if he did find the balsam, and what if he did somehow carve it into a shoe? What could a princess ever see to desire in a poor apothecary anyhow? He didn't know the first thing about running a kingdom. The only thing he could offer—besides some handy knowledge about the preservation and uses of herbs and minerals—was himself.

And what good was that?

The looming question, really, was what he should do. The king had threatened punishment if he failed to come through. And just as all those mocking courtiers had predicted, he had failed the king. He had failed the princess.

But perhaps...perhaps he didn't need to return. Really, what was there in his hometown that he couldn't find elsewhere? He was skilled enough to find work in another kingdom. And yet...

He had promised. He also needed to return the borrowed horse. And he needed to see Princess River one more time.

Besides, Elliot thought as he kicked aside a dead branch. He'd taken a risk. Sometimes risks didn't pay. There wasn't much more he could do than to face the king like a man.

He searched for the rest of the morning and into the afternoon. But just as on all the other days, he found nothing but spruces, spruces, and more spruces. Disappointment settled over him like a suffocating cloud as he stopped walking and looked up at the sun, which was setting through the trees.

"Well," he said to Sir Luke, who had been hopping

behind him. "I think it's time we have some dinner." He took a step toward the horse to unpack the saddlebag when the rabbit leaped in front of him. Elliot let out a surprised yell as he tried not to step on the little animal, and he fell hard on the ground, a sharp pain moving through his elbow.

"Luke!" he gasped as he pushed himself up. "What was..." But the words died on his lips. An aroma, faint but familiar, wafted toward him. It smelled like...cinnamon.

Nearly mad with impossible hope, Elliot scrambled onto his hands and knees and crawled on all fours, sniffing. Whenever the scent disappeared, he retreated until he smelled it again, until, just as the sun dipped beneath the horizon, he found it.

The tree was much smaller than he'd been searching for. It was somewhere between white and gray, and unlike the spruce trees, its trunk was smooth rather than scaly.

The tree was young, so young that even in his fit of madness, Elliot hated to kill it. Who knew if there was another like it in the forest? But he needed the wood to cure the king. And the king was more important than any tree.

Making a truce with himself, Elliot took a few cones from the tree and tossed them around him so they would remain in the wood. Then he took a few more and slipped them into his pocket. If he could grow more of these trees at home, he would be able to cure far more people than just the king.

Then he cut the tree down, making sure to leave part of the stump to grow back. His uncle had taught him enough of plant husbandry to know that trees like the balsam could potentially grow back if given enough time. Finally, with a palpitating heart and a mind nearly blank from shock, he made his bed on the ground for one more night.

"Tomorrow," he told Sir Luke, who was lazily munching a flower, "we go home."

CHAPTER
SIXTEEN

Elliot arrived home the evening of the fourth day after finding the balsam. Thankfully, there hadn't been any fairy rings or violent storms on the return trip. But the king's horse was tired, and Elliot forced himself to slow and clean and feed the poor animal in Lord Gaskin's stables before retreating to his cottage and pulling the treasure from his bag.

The wood was beautiful, so white it nearly glittered in the light of his small hearth. But how to make it into a shoe...

Elliot took a shaky breath and prayed for a miracle.

He knew that to shape the wood, he would need to soften it. At least...he was pretty sure that's what he needed to do. He'd watched a neighboring shoemaker several times as a boy, and the craft had fascinated him. He distinctly remembered watching the shoemaker boil the wood. Or was it the leather?

Whichever it was, there was only enough wood to make one shoe, so he couldn't make a mistake. Perhaps he should wait until the morning. He was just as tired as his horse, and he was nearly seeing double. But no. His audience with the king was tomorrow. He could sleep when it was all done. After all, he thought wryly, if this went wrong, that was about all one could do in prison, he supposed. And if he was dead, he wouldn't need sleep at all. So he pushed through the fatigue and forced himself to not only boil the water in his cauldron but to put the wood in.

Just a little while, he told himself. Then the wood would soften enough for him to carve it. At least, he hoped that's how it would work. But he could think about that when it was done. For now, he would simply watch and wait.

E lliot awakened to a strange smell. His whole body felt as though a giant had stomped on it, and he was still at his table. The sky outside showed signs of morning light.

Morning light.

The morning of the day he would see the king.

Panic and dread froze Elliot in place until he smelled again whatever had awakened him. But this scent only threw him into a deeper panic as he realized it was the smell of burning wood. Jumping up so fast he knocked his stool over, he ran to the cauldron and stared down in horror.

He hadn't just softened the wood. He'd boiled all of the water out. And not only had the water boiled out, but the wood was no longer even wood.

It had crystallized into a substance no bigger than his thumb.

This was the end. The Almighty God had not only given him this chance to go on the journey, but He had even provided Elliot the wood–this mythical, miracle wood–with which to cure the king and gain the hand of the woman he loved.

And Elliot had ruined it all for sleep.

Elliot stepped outside and vomited behind the corner of the cottage. He could chew some of the peppermint growing nearby, but he had no desire to alleviate his suffering. He had been his own downfall. And now, he would most likely pay with his life.

He walked back into the cottage as though wandering through a nightmare. And it was a nightmare. Just the kind he couldn't awaken from.

Seized by a rage which he'd never felt before, he grabbed the cauldron from the pot, burning his fingers in the process. Throwing it on the ground, he glowered down at the brown crystals. How dare they mock him? As if he didn't have enough to mourn? Why couldn't they have burned out with the water? Why did they have to taunt him in his agony?

He reached down with stinging hands and took hold of the largest piece of crystal. He had meant to throw it back into the fire, but the moment his fingers touched the crystal, he froze and then let out a shout as it slipped back down into the cauldron. Then, slowly, he held up his hand.

The fingers that had touched the crystal were healed of their burns. Wholly and completely healed. The fingers that had throbbed and turned scarlet red looked as though he'd never grabbed the cauldron at all.

A new determination pulsed through him as he grabbed his tools out of his still packed bag and began carefully scraping the bottom of the cauldron, determined not to lose a single piece. Then he took his mortar and pestle and began crushing the crystal into powder.

The bells tolled as he worked, reminding him that he didn't have much time. Frantically, he poured the crystal powder into a small glass vial.

A knock sounded at the door.

"Elliot?" Lord Gaskin called, his voice muffled through the wood. "The king's men are here to escort you to the palace."

"I...I'll be there in just a moment!" Elliot called out, his voice shaking. He grabbed his jar of aloe and jabbed some into the vial with the powder. Then he snatched up a wooden stirring dowel and began to mix.

"They seem impatient, Elliot," His Grace called again.

"I'm ready!" Elliot called. He threw on his cloak and tucked the vial into his bag. And though he smiled at Lord Gaskin, a dead weight settled in the pit of his stomach. There was no time to see if his concoction had worked. Not even time to test it on his other fingers. All that was left of his hopes and dreams sat in the bag that rested on his thigh as he followed the guards to the stable to pick up the king's horse, and then to the palace one last time.

CHAPTER
SEVENTEEN

E lliot did his best to block out the mocking and jeers as they neared the palace. His hope was riding on the small vial in his bag. If it failed, he would deserve the mocking. But if he succeeded...

As he was escorted through the palace doors into the grand entrance, he did his best to steel himself for what was inevitable.

He might have let himself hope before, but now as he walked upon the polished stone floors, more aware than ever of the disparity between himself and the princess, he knew the truth.

Princess River couldn't ever really mean to take him as her own. At least, she could never want to. Not after being sought after by men of royal and noble lines her entire life. And even if the king insisted they marry, Elliot knew in his heart of hearts that he could never ask her to pledge herself to him against her will.

Perhaps the king would grant him a little land and enough money to start his own apothecary. But more important than that, however, would be that for one moment...one fleeting moment, Princess River would look upon him. And she would *see*.

His heart beat so fast he grew dizzy as he entered the king's chamber for a second time. Waiting for him were people crammed into every inch of the room. But his heart sank just as fast when he realized that the princess was not one of them.

Surely, she would be there to see her father's possible healing?

But maybe it was better this way, he reflected as he was directed to stand at the foot of the king's bed. If he failed, she wouldn't be there to watch.

"Don't let him do it!" a man shouted.

Elliot looked up to see the prince–the one who had been standing with Princess River last time–burst into the room. His face was red and contorted with anger.

"I have it on good authority that he means to kill you, Your Majesty!" the prince continued.

"Based on whose witness?" the king asked with a tired sigh.

Elliot did his best to stand tall and look unruffled, but it was difficult. This man obviously saw him as a rival. And in no way could Elliot compete with a prince.

"A fairy! In the woods! We attempted to catch him with a fairy ring, but–"

"So River was right," the king said, pushing himself slightly higher on his pillows. "You did try to cheat."

Elliot stared at the king and then the foreign prince. *He* had been the reason Elliot had been stuck in a fairy ring?

"Your Majesty, if you mean to let–"

"Sit *down*, Avery!" the king snapped. "And shut up. You may learn something." His frown deepened. "And don't think I won't be talking to your father and brother about this."

The prince paled before retreating to the door. Shaking his head, the king looked up at Elliot once again. "As I was about to ask before being so rudely interrupted, did you make the shoe?" the king asked. His face seemed paler than it had two weeks before, and his voice was more breathy.

Elliot licked his lips before speaking. "I...I did not, Sire."

The king's brows furrowed, so Elliot rushed on.

"I must also confess, Sire, that I lied. About being a shoe-maker, I mean. I'm an apothecary."

The room burst into a roar of whispers, but the king merely looked surprised. "Why would you lie about such a thing? I would have felt more confident had an apothecary come to me in the first place."

Elliot nodded. "It was foolish, I know. And I'm sorry. Deeply sorry. But I feared retribution for not coming forth sooner with a cure. I told the truth when I said that I had only just discovered it in the book when I came to you." He had to pause to catch his breath. "You asked for a shoe. I was afraid you wouldn't give me a chance if I told you I'd never made a shoe in my life."

The king tilted his head. Elliot waited for the moment the king would tell the guards to deliver Elliot's head to him on a platter, but instead, the king took a deep breath. "Why are you telling me this now, young man?"

"Because," Elliot said, slipping the strap of his bag over his head, "I wanted to be forthright. It's how my father raised me. And...while I wasn't able to make the shoe, I have something else."

"You ought to be hanged and left out for the birds!" one of the women called out.

"No one lies to the king!" someone else shouted.

But the king held up a hand, and the shouting ceased. "Well, what are you waiting for?" he asked.

If Elliot was honest, he'd been waiting for the order to be given that would result in his execution.

"If you haven't noticed," the king said with a dry smile, "I'm not at liberty to be particular at the moment."

Elliot stared at him for a few long seconds, then let out a rather pained laugh. Then he pulled the vial out of his bag, and with shaking hands, opened the stopper.

Next, he removed the king's bandage. It took all his uncle's training not to fall back and gag. The wound was festering, yellow and brown, and it smelled worse than anything Elliot had ever smelled in his life. But a good apothecary didn't react to the wound. His duty was to heal.

Using a dowel, he began to apply the salve to the king's foot. He said prayer after prayer as he gently rubbed the salve over every part of the injury. When he finished the most infected area, he began to work the salve into the outer edges of the wound. Only when he was done did he glance up at the king.

He'd been expecting a cry of pain. Or a groan or some other sound to indicate the king's status. But instead of a shout or other expression of pain, the king was silent, tears streaming down his grizzled cheeks.

"Your Majesty?" one of the court physicians, easily identifiable by his physician's symbol--a leaf and a bone--sewn into his cloak, stepped forward. "Are you well?"

"I..." the king paused and shuddered. "I can't feel...I can't feel the pain!"

There was a long silence before the court physicians erupted into loud conversation.

"The king can't feel anything!" one of them shouted at Elliot. "This is your fault!"

Rough hands grabbed Elliot's arms, and he stood there helpless as the king made waving motions with his hands and arms.

"Shut up, you fools!" he was shouting over the din. "I didn't say I was losing my sense of touch! I *meant* that that pain is gone!

A collective gasp went up from the crowd. Elliot dared to look back down at the king's foot and found himself surrounded by five physicians. Sure enough, just as with his burnt fingers, the king's foot was as good as new.

Joyful chaos broke out, and Elliot found himself shoved to the back of the room as more and more people tried to see the king. As he was pushed out of the throng, Elliot used the time to search for the princess, but after several moments of nearly being trampled, he knew for certain that she wasn't there.

His chest felt tight as he made his way out of the palace and back to Lord Gaskin's house. Part of him knew he should return to the palace and await the king's notice, but the other part of him...the heart that seemed incapable of beating properly, pushed him onward.

He'd known, just as everyone else had, that the princess had intended to marry the second prince of their neighboring kingdom to the north--the rude prince, it seemed, who had annoyed the king this morning. The union would have made sense. The two kingdoms were allies, and from what Elliot understood, the young prince and princess had spent much time together as they grew. Their fathers were good friends, and as Prince Avery was a second son, that he would join Princess River in her own kingdom seemed the most likely solution, pleasing everyone involved.

And yet, Elliot had hoped for just a few moments that the princess might look outside of the spoiled prince at someone else. There was no greater act Elliot could undertake to prove his affection. Not even Prince Avery could do what he had done.

And yet, the princess hadn't even deigned to look upon him.

"Elliot!"

Elliot looked up to see his employer hurrying after him. He stopped and waited for Lord Gaskin to join him. He wondered if Lord Gaskin might be angry with him. Or jealous. But to his surprise, his employer looked...happy. And confused.

"Your Grace?" he asked.

"What are you doing here?" Lord Gaskin nodded at his home, which was only a few houses away. "You just cured the king! Surely you haven't forgotten what he promised you!"

Elliot forced a smile. "No, Your Grace. I haven't forgotten."

"Then why are you out here? The king was looking for you. I went out to find you for him."

Elliot took a deep breath and sighed. "Your Grace, when you fell in love with Lady Lindsay...did she wish to marry you?"

The lord's confusion slowly softened into a sad smile. "She did."

"It was arranged, though, wasn't it?" Elliot asked.

Lord Gaskin nodded. "It was."

"But if she hadn't wanted to marry you..." Elliot let his words trail off, and Lord Gaskin let out a sigh.

"You believe the princess doesn't want to marry you," he said slowly.

Elliot tried swallowing the lump in his throat. "I love her. I've loved her since she showed me kindness when we were children. She doesn't remember me, of course. But I was hoping if..." He shook his head. "She didn't even come to see her father healed today."

Lord Gaskin's brow furrowed. "It's not a secret that the princess has been angry with her father for writing the edict. Although, I will tell you that she's been incredibly busy as of late. There are any number of reasons she might have missed this morning."

But Elliot just shook his head. "Love means sacrificing my own desires for hers. And if she wants to marry Prince Avery..." He straightened. "I'll honor that."

Lord Gaskin's mouth fell slightly open. "But the riches. The elevation. If anyone deserves that, I'll be the first to vouch that it's you! I'm sure the king would at least honor that part of his edict even if you do not wish to press the princess for her hand."

Elliot gave him a sad smile. "I didn't do it for those."

Lord Gaskin was quiet for a moment, and Elliot felt that, although they were standing in the middle of the street, the rest of the world had faded away. Lord Gaskin had always been kind to him, if a bit cheap. But Elliot had never imagined him to be so understanding.

But then again, if Elliot knew anything about his employer, it was that Lord Gaskin loved Lady Lindsay with all his heart.

"Go home," Lord Gaskin finally said in a soft voice. "Rest. I'll speak to the king. I'm sure we'll find out where the princess has gone."

Elliot bowed his head. "Thank you, Your Grace."

Lord Gaskin put his hand on Elliot's shoulder. "Whether you become my king or remain my apothecary, I am glad to have known you, Elliot. You're a rare sort of man, and I wish there were more like you."

Warmed by Lord Gaskin's praise and feeling more

hollow inside than ever, Elliot finished his trek back to his cottage. He really was tired, and perhaps a long sleep would restore some sunshine back into his life. Raindrops were beginning to sprinkle the ground, and the wind was picking up as exhaustion from the last two weeks began to truly haunt him. But as he reached his doorstep, something sparkly caught his eye.

Bending down, he found a polished pink stone on his doorstep. He picked it up and stared at it. Where could this have...

Understanding hit him, and before he knew it, he was racing through the rain toward the river.

T he rain wasn't hard, but it was coming down steadily by the time Elliot neared the bend in the river. And there, standing on the little hill above the bank, was the princess.

Her hair, which must have been carefully piled on her head and pinned into place that morning, had tendrils blowing in the breeze, but the imperfection only made her more beautiful. Most of all, though, her big hazel eyes were focused on him.

"All this time," she called over the sound of the river below and the wind in the trees. "You were the one waiting for me."

He walked up the hill carefully, feeling a little as though he were approaching a rabbit that might streak away if he moved too fast. Then, suddenly, they were face-to-face.

"I...I knew I had no right to hope," he said. How in the world had she known? Not only had she found his cottage, but she seemed to recognize him. Was it possible? After all these years?

She came closer, closer until their faces were only inches apart, her bright eyes gazing fiercely up into his. "Tell me," she said, her lips distractingly close. "If we were to marry today, what would your first edict be?"

He blinked at her. "Um, edict?"

The right corner of her lips twitched. "Your first official order."

"Um," he scratched his neck. "I don't know about my first order. I'd have to learn about all that. But would it be too much to ask for a place to put my books?" He paused. "And maybe some combat lessons." He shrugged and gave her a stupid grin. "I'm afraid the milkmaid might be able to best me in a duel, and that wouldn't be very becoming in a king, should I ever be called upon to lead troops."

The princess was smiling now. But she stayed silent, so he bumbled on like an idiot.

"The palace does have a library, doesn't it? I could study up on the art of war while I was at it. And civics and law and..." He trailed off. Her eyes hadn't left his face. How were they so colorful? Shards of green, blue, yellow, and even red wrapped in a ring of golden brown. So long had he dreamed of this moment, and now he didn't really know what to do with it. Still, she didn't speak, so he held up the pink rock.

"I'm sorry I didn't check the boulder. I was going to bring you a sachet of wildflowers, but–"

His rambling was interrupted when she put her hands on his face and pulled it down toward hers. Then her lips met his.

Elliot had never let himself imagine the princess's kiss, but his dreams had sometimes defied him. But this...this was so much better than his unconscious had ever imagined. Her mouth was soft and careful, but he could feel the passion within them nevertheless. That passion unlocked something inside of him, and he let instinct take over. He drew her close, and his own desire poured forth. Pressing one hand against the small of her back, he pulled her against him more tightly and kissed her until she sighed and leaned into him. Warm rain fell softly on their hair and faces. And as she snuggled up against his chest, her head tucked into his neck, he marveled.

Through some miracle, Princess River was his.

"I can't believe you remembered me," he murmured. "It's been so long."

He could feel her smile into his neck. "I had a little help."

He pulled back to look at her. "From whom?"

She grinned, and her eyes sparkled. Would he really get to look into those eyes for the rest of his days? "I know people." Then she laughed. "I also hope to become better acquainted with Madam Balastrade in particular. I think she would be an excellent adviser to the crown."

Elliot stared at her for a long moment before throwing his head back and laughing. As he did, the clouds above broke apart to leak sunshine down upon the river and over the meadow around them.

"But it all came back to you," Princess River said, leaning her head on his shoulder again. "When I saw you, I knew I had seen you before. And it bothered me that I didn't know where."

"But...what about this?" he gestured to the rock. "How did you know that was me?"

She smiled. "For a long time, I was sure it was someone else."

Elliot made a face. "I guessed."

Her smile only grew, her pink lips distracting him, smooth and soft in the tentative sunlight.

"But then I found this."

To his disappointment, she backed up. But when she pulled a small scrap of paper from her reticule, he sucked in a quick breath. His hand shook slightly as she handed him the sketch.

It wasn't one of his best. He'd nearly given it to her several times, though, at the river. But each time he'd been tempted, fear had gotten the better of him. He'd known that when she saw it, she would learn the truth.

"I was afraid you might be angry if you found out," he said, watching her warily.

Her eyes widened. "Angry? Why?"

He shrugged. "I'm not exactly nobility. I thought... perhaps you would be upset that your correspondence was with a commoner." He cleared his throat. "I was convinced you believed the presents were from the prince."

She nodded slowly. "I did. But the longer we went on, the more Avery showed me who he truly is...and who he is not." She gave Elliot a wan smile. "I just wasn't wise enough to see it." Then she bent down and pulled something out from beneath the boulder. When she straightened again, she was holding a small chest. When she opened it, his mouth fell open. For there in the chest was every single one of his gifts.

"Put it in," she said with a smile. "Add to my treasure."

As if in a dream, he put the drawing in the box. As he did, his eyes began to sting, and his chest constricted.

She put the box down quickly. "What's the matter?" she asked, taking his face in her hands again.

He shook his head, his thoughts bouncing around in his head, painfully aware of every single one of her fingers. "I'm sorry. I just..." His voice fell to a whisper. "I came to the palace knowing I could never deserve you."

She stepped closer again. "Then why did you try?" she whispered back. "If you thought you couldn't?"

"Because," he answered, his voice sounding unusually low. "I just wanted to see you smile."

That earned him another kiss.

EPILOGUE

River's father cracked the door open and poked his head through. "Is she ready yet?"

"No, and she won't ever be ready if you don't quit distracting everyone in here!" River's aunt moved to shut the door again, but her father stuck his boot in the opening and grinned.

"Just need to make sure my grandchildren–"

"Like I said, you'll never get any grandchildren if you don't let your daughter finish getting ready for her wedding! Now shoo!" River's aunt said, managing to shut the door and lock it behind her. River grinned as her aunt rolled her eyes. No one else in the kingdom would dare shoo the king, but then again, his sister-in-law wasn't like anyone else in the kingdom.

"You look radiant!" her aunt said as she walked back to River, taking River's hands, her eyes glistening. "Your mother..." She put a hand over her mouth and lowered her head, silent sobs shaking her shoulders.

River wrapped her arms around her aunt, her own eyes pricking. "I know," she whispered into her aunt's hair. "I wish she was here, too."

"You look just like her," her aunt said, looking up and touching River's cheek. "I thought I'd never see her again, but when I look at you, it's like she's here all over."

River opened her mouth to respond, but they were interrupted by another knock on the door. Beth went to answer it. She listened to whoever was on the other side, then shut the door and hurried back.

"The groom is ready," she said with a curtsey.

"Oh my," River's aunt said, accepting the handkerchief proffered by one of the servants. "I'm going to make you late. And you can't cry. Your face is a work of art."

River laughed, the sting leaving her eyes slightly.

"Come, come," her aunt said, taking River's arm in hers. "Let's go before your father shows up again. I don't think my husband can hold him off much longer."

River made her way to the palace chapel, but to her surprise, the halls that should have been empty weren't. Servants lined the halls, each bowing or curtseying as she passed, each with a smile or whispered blessing.

"I didn't expect that," River whispered to her aunt when they finally stood before the chapel's towering oak doors.

River's aunt turned her so they were face-to-face. "You've doubted your place for a long time," she said with a gentle smile. River stared at her. "And...everyone knew that?"

That was embarrassing.

River's aunt chuckled. "River, they've watched you grow up. And even though you didn't know it, *they* have known you were ready for a long time."

"Ready for what?" River asked.

"To rule."

"But my father—"

"Is still as alive and obnoxious as ever, yes. But I think this was the Almighty God's way of proving to you that this is your place. And when He calls your father home, you'll be exactly where you're supposed to be." She glanced at the doors, and her smile widened. "And *with* the man you were created for and he for you."

River's father appeared at their side, as strong and hand-some as ever, without even the slightest sign of a limp. He held out his arm, and River took it.

"Are you ready?" he asked gently.

Not trusting herself to speak, River merely nodded. Then she stretched up on the tips of her toes and kissed his whiskered cheek.

"What was that for?" he asked with a surprised grin.

She smiled back. "For seeing what I couldn't. Even when I didn't want to hear the truth." She bumped him slightly with her shoulder. "Although, I will admit that I'm quite relieved your hero wasn't someone Grandfather's age."

He coughed. "I didn't tell you at the time, but I might

have added several addendums to the edict that would have prevented certain...undesirables from success."

River's mouth dropped open. "And you didn't tell me?" she hissed.

The king chuckled. "What fun would that have been?"

She glared at her father, but when his merry eyes met hers, she chuckled, too. Then she straightened her shoulders and waited for the doors to open. And as she did, the reality of what she was about to do crashed down on her.

She was getting married.

If she was honest, she'd been putting off thoughts of her wedding for the last three months. It was easier than she would have thought, largely for two reasons. First, her father had sent Prince Avery home with a strongly worded letter to his father and elder brother, and River hadn't seen him since. Second, because Elliot hadn't been present at the palace more than one or two days before being whisked away again. Her father's general had taken one look at him the day after he'd moved in and had nearly gone into a state of shock. With the king's permission, he'd immediately dragged Elliot to the soldiers' training camp in the woods. They hadn't even given him time enough to write letters.

Life without her betrothed had been...strange for River. On one hand, she found that she missed him. She missed finding his little gifts and poems, and she missed leaving her own. She longed to ask him questions and get to know the man who had loved her since she was a girl.

But she found with some guilt that she was also some-what relieved that he was gone. Then she didn't have to struggle with being perfectly aware of just how intimate their old but delicate friendship was going to get. In one sense, she'd known him for years. He'd proved himself faithful in every way imaginable, from loving her in the little ways to risking his life to save her father. But marriage...

Marriage meant far more than giving him her attention. It meant giving him everything.

Was she ready to give him everything?

The doors opened before she could answer her own question. Music played as the choir sang, and everyone within the doors was standing and had their eyes on her. White flowers covered the chapel like snow, and crystals hung in the ceiling-high windows filled the chapel with sparkles. But River saw little of that.

All she saw was him.

The young man at the end of the aisle was hardly recognizable. He was still thin, but his chest now filled out his new military uniform, the gold buttons on his breast glinting in the light.

Avery's buttons had only ever been silver.

His hair was cut shorter, much closer to his head, and now he stood erect, not hunching as he had the first time he'd entered the palace. He wore his sword and scabbard well. And his eyes were focused on her.

River couldn't say why precisely, but there was a fire in those eyes that put her remaining fears to rest. It was a determination she'd never seen in Avery's eyes. And that fiery gaze was all for her.

When her father began leading her down the aisle to the

holy man, River suddenly felt as though she were flying. And when her father placed her hand on Elliot's outstretched one, a shiver ran up her arm and down her spine. His fingers were indeed calloused as she had imagined. But they were gentle against hers.

River shivered again, but this time, from desire, a kind of longing she'd never known before.

The wedding sped by, and so did the magnificent reception her aunt had planned. They ate and drank and danced and greeted so many people that River soon lost track of who was there. But eventually, the clock struck midnight, and River nodded to her aunt, who gave her a nod in return. Then River took her husband's hand and pulled him toward a side door and down several servants' corridors before they finally reached their new chambers.

Neither of them spoke as Elliot locked the door behind them, and suddenly, River was far too hot. So hot that she wondered if she might faint.

When he turned around from locking the door, Elliot took one look at her and took her hand again. "Let's get some fresh air," he said gently, tugging her toward the balcony. River followed with unspoken thanks as he opened the doors and led her outside.

The moon was full, and the river glistened brightly as it snaked along the palace's boundary. Several fisherman's boats moved silently down its bends, black against the glittering ripples below.

"I know...I know this was fast," Elliot said, turning to

face her. "And I want you to know that whatever you feel comfortable with, I'm just glad to be here."

River watched him silently, unable to make sense of the emotions swirling around in her head. But he didn't seem to notice. Instead, he gently pushed a lock of hair behind her ear.

"I just can't believe you're mine," he whispered. "I knew I could never deserve you."

River should have answered, but she found herself distracted by the mesmerizing way his jaw moved when he spoke. It was a strong jaw with good angles, and she had the sudden urge to touch it.

So she did.

His eyes closed, and he sighed as she gently ran her fingers down his face.

"When we first spoke...back on the bank," she said softly, "You said that then, too." She traced his temple. "Why wouldn't you deserve me?"

He opened his eyes and looked down into hers. "You're a princess. You deserve everything beautiful and good in the world. And all I have to give is..." He gestured down at his body. "Me."

Whether it was the humility that Avery had always lacked or the sweetness in Elliot's gaze, River could never say. But a boldness suddenly seized her, and she took a step forward so she could place her hands on his chest.

"True as that may be," she said, marveling at the way it felt to touch him, "I've seen enough to expect a lot of you, Prince Elliot."

He took her waist in his left hand and held her face with his right. Then slowly, carefully, he pressed his lips against hers.

His kiss was like sunshine wrapped in honey, and when she opened her eyes again, she was surprised to see that it was still night.

"I shall try to please my princess," he said in a throaty voice.

She turned so that her back was pressed up against him and she was facing the night. It was easier to focus on what she was saying when she wasn't looking into his eyes as well. "You can please me with your friendship," she said, "and your continued bookishness. For the sake of the kingdom, of course."

He ran his nose down the back of her neck, making her tremble. "Of course," he whispered.

She took one of his hands and pressed it against her belly. "Children, obviously."

He stilled for a moment before his hold on her tightened. "As many as you'd like."

Then she turned once more and took his face in her hands. "And you. Just you."

"Only," he said, bending until his mouth brushed hers, "if you'll be mine in return." Then he pulled her into a stronger, deeper kiss than any he'd given her before.

She smiled into his kiss. "Always and forevermore."

The Prince's Dangerous Wish

A Nevertold Fairy Tale Novella, Book #2

Nadine had a decent idea of what her son's gift was from an early age. She wondered years later why the magic changed, requiring him to use particular words once he was verbal, but allowing him more variance when he was small. It mattered little, though, for once he was able to speak, her fears were confirmed. The faerie hadn't been exaggerating the danger her gift brought with it, and not much time passed before Nadine would have done nearly anything to give the gift back.

Rolf had the sweetest disposition Nadine had ever seen in a baby, which was probably why the palace didn't burn down during his first two years of life. He cried as often as any infant, but his tantrums were few and far between, much to his mother's great relief. Unfortunately, just before his first birthday, Nadine was forced to admit that what she feared most was really true.

The boy had been playing quietly on the rug beside his mother as she penned a letter to a cousin, excusing their lack of attendance at the cousin's wedding by citing her son's fragile health, the general excuse that allowed her to keep him away from the court and other large gatherings.

"No one who saw you for more than five minutes would believe it." Nadine looked over at him with a wry smile. "You are the strongest, healthiest little boy I've ever seen."

Rolf looked up at her and gurgled at her through a big, drooly grin.

"And I do hate to lie," she murmured, looking back at the letter. "But I don't know how to explain the truth." She peeked back at her son again. "You truly leave me without words."

To explain that her son was faerie gifted would be nothing less than to invite trouble, especially as faeries had so rarely blessed the children of her husband's line.

"Mama," he said, holding his chubby little hands out to her.

"Just a moment, darling," she said distantly, reading over her letter again.

"Mama!" he said again. But this time, it was not a request. It was very similar to the tone his father used when issuing orders in the throne room. Nadine let out a little scream as her chair tipped her sideways, dumping her onto the floor beside the baby and spilling the bottle of ink in her lap. She was still staring open-mouthed at the mess when Alicia rushed in.

"Is everything–Your Highness! Are you well?" She hurried to help Nadine to her feet.

"Um, yes. I mean, please get me some water," Nadine said, trying to sound more coherent than she felt. "I...I think I feel a little faint."

Alicia called one of the younger ladies-in-waiting from the next room and doled out orders quickly. In no time at all, Nadine was clean and wore a new dress, and the dirtied rug had already been replaced with a new one.

"Did you do that?" Nadine whispered to her son when they were finally alone again.

He just laughed and shook his little wooden rattle.

Before Nadine could collect her thoughts, a knock sounded at the door. Without waiting for Nadine's answer, the door burst open, and a stately woman with black and silver hair and many jewels walked in.

"Lavinia—" Nadine began, immediately moving her child to her hip. "How can I help you?" How did her mother-in-law always choose to find the worst time for everything?

"I've come for the child," the queen mother said, looking Nadine up and down. As always, Nadine suddenly felt quite shabby.

"Whatever for?" she asked, trying not to sound flustered as Rolf began chewing on her lace collar.

"You had a fall," Lavinia said evenly. "I have come to take him so you can rest."

"Oh....oh, that's quite sweet of you. Very thoughtful indeed. But I'm well enough, thank you. I had just been sitting too long, and I stood too quickly."

"I told my son you weren't the hardiest of stock," Lavina said coolly. "Come, give him here. Albert is in a meeting and needn't hear of this." She held out her arms just as Rolf had done to Nadine an hour before.

"I thank you," Nadine said, thinking quickly. "But I shall keep him with me. In fact, we'll be going to his wet nurse soon, and I promised him we would stop by the menagerie on the way."

"What, and touch those filthy animals?" the queen mother looked appalled. "Really, Nadine, have some sense."

Nadine hesitated. She was in dangerous waters here. Albert doted on both his wife and his son. But he was as dutiful to his mother as any son had ever been. And he valued her opinion over nearly anyone else's. Which would have been lovely if she hadn't seemed to think Nadine a peculiar girl from the outset, and determined to remind her son of this conviction every chance she got.

Nadine looked down into Rolf's deep blue eyes. He gazed back at her, his face full of trust and adoration.

She felt her will harden.

"No, I'll take him with me." She stalked toward the door. "Alicia, dear. I'm going out."

Alicia appeared with a tray of tea. But as soon as she understood what Nadine wanted, she readied herself to go outside and followed Nadine obediently, pausing only to glance between Nadine and her mother-in-law once before shutting the door behind her. Nadine felt as though she could still feel her mother-in-law's razor sharp gaze through the door.

"Your Highness," Alicia whispered as soon as they were in the menagerie. "Is there any way I can be of assistance?"

Nadine was about to respond with a no, but then she stopped. It was undeniable now that the faerie had gifted her son—cursed was more like it—to receive anything he wished. She'd wondered several times before when he had pointed and uttered a gurgled word here or there, but this morning, his word had been clear and commanding.

This was a nightmare.

Even the mere consideration of what his life would be like was enough to make her feel dizzy. Albert, while mercifully a good king, was already used to getting his way. And he didn't get even half the things he wished for. How was her son supposed to survive his early years? His childhood? His adolescence, getting everything he ever desired? Such evil would kill the boy, and possibly a good deal of those around him.

What had the faerie been thinking?

Find out just what the faerie was thinking and whether Rolf gets his happily-ever-after in the next book, The Prince's Dangerous Wish: A Clean Fairy Tale Retelling of The Pink.

§

Dear Reader,
Thank you for reading The White Slipper.
If you'd like more (free) happily-ever-afters, visit BrittanyFichterFiction.com, where my subscribers get free, exclusive stories (like the ones below), sneak peeks at books before they're published, coupon codes, and much more.

Also, if you liked the book, it would be a huge help to me if you could leave an honest review on your favorite ebook retailer or Goodreads so others can find this story, too!

About the Author

Brittany lives with her Prince Charming, their little fairy, and their little prince in a ~~sparkling~~ (decently clean) castle in whatever kingdom the Air Force has most recently placed them. When she's not writing, Brittany can be found chasing her kids around with a DSLR and belting it in the church choir.

Subscribe: BrittanyFichterFiction.com
Email: BrittanyFichterFiction@gmail.com
Facebook: Facebook.com/BFichterFiction
Instagram: @BrittanyFichterFiction

THE WHITE SLIPPER: A CLEAN FAIRY TALE RETELLING OF
THE WHITE SLIPPER

Copyright © 2022 Brittany Fichter

Brittany Fichter. -- 1st ed.

Cover Design by Moor Books Design

Edited by Theresa Emms